"You're tying a *bib* on my bulldog?"

Dave stared at Jenny, horrified at the sight of poor Jake. "Dogs drool. It's what they do."

"Not on my Princess!" Jenny furiously finished tying the knot, then marched back into her store clutching her poodle. The man was impossible! Infuriating! Maddening!

And so incredibly handsome, she wondered if she'd lost her mind. What *was* she doing, ruining an opportunity for a budding relationship?

She stuck her head out the door. "Dave!" she yelled. "Coffee tonight? Seven?"

"All right." He scowled at her. "Make it dinner. My treat."

"Fine!"

"Fine!"

Jenny slammed the screen door. *Well.* She expelled a breath of relief. *They had a date tonight.*

Dear Reader,

I'm pleased to welcome back Lori Copeland with *Fudgeballs and Other Sweets*. She is one of the original launch authors for Love & Laughter as well as an award-winning author for writing humor. *Publishers Weekly* had this to say recently about her work: "Copeland has a winner in this crisply written, sweetly sentimental tale of love lost and found." With Lori's name on the cover, you know you're in for a good read and a good time! Plus the story features two cute and memorable dogs—could you ask for more?

Valerie Kirkwood also has written her second book for us, *Rent-a-Friend.* The poor heroine has been badly betrayed by her best friend, and she's vowed not to have any more friends—*ever!* But that just doesn't work, so she decides to take the intelligent route, one most women can relate to very easily: she goes *shopping* for a friend.

As an interesting aside, both Lori and Valerie also write historical romances. Clearly a talented pair!

So relax and enjoy a chuckle.

Malle Vallik

Malle Vallik
Associate Senior Editor

Lori Copeland
FUDGEBALLS AND OTHER SWEETS

Harlequin Books

TORONTO • NEW YORK • LONDON
AMSTERDAM • PARIS • SYDNEY • HAMBURG
STOCKHOLM • ATHENS • TOKYO • MILAN
MADRID • WARSAW • BUDAPEST • AUCKLAND

ISBN 0-373-44041-3

FUDGEBALLS AND OTHER SWEETS

Bestselling author **Lori Copeland** has published over forty novels in the past thirteen years. Her quick wit and humor have been much rewarded: she is the recipient of the prestigious *Romantic Times* Reviewer's Choice and Career Achievement awards, as well as the *Affaire de Coeur* Gold and Silver Certificate awards.

Lori loves writing. And she believes that love and laughter are a natural pairing—"No matter what the situation, or who my characters are, I can't help but look on the lighter side of life. Of course, chocolate helps!"

Her recent trip to Mackinaw Island was a delight and an inspiration for *Fudgeballs and Other Sweets*. Look for Lori's next Love & Laughter title, *Fruitcakes and Other Leftovers,* in your favorite bookstore Christmas 1998.

Books by Lori Copeland

HARLEQUIN LOVE & LAUGHTER
2—DATES AND OTHER NUTS

Don't miss any of our special offers. Write to us at the following address for information on our newest releases.

Harlequin Reader Service
U.S.: 3010 Walden Ave., P.O. Box 1325, Buffalo, NY 14269
Canadian: P.O. Box 609, Fort Erie, Ont. L2A 5X3

1

—————

ROUSED FROM A DEEP SLEEP, Jake snapped his head up. When he saw it was the poodle causing the racket that had disturbed him, he snorted and smacked his lips. Tucking his head between his paws, he yawned, then closed his eyes. Yip, yip, yip. If he had a bone for every time that fuzzy-headed broad said yip, he'd be the richest bulldog on Mackinac Island.

Hoo, boy. Nature calling. Rolling his eyes, he shoved himself to his feet. Seconds later, he scratched the grass with his hind leg to cover the soiled area, glancing up when the yipping suddenly stopped. "What?" he demanded. The poodle was looking at him as if he'd just hacked up a bone.

The highly strung dog's nose quivered with disdain. "Monsieur, I hope you didn't do what I think you did."

Jake circled the tree to which he and Princess were tethered. "Yeah, like I'm gonna hold it till my eyeballs float? You just stay on your side of the tree, I'll stay on mine." He hated pushy women. His life had been much better when it was just him and his human, Dave.

Princess chanced a quick glance at Jake. Short, stocky, built like a prizefighter. *Ooh, la, la, what an* amant—*but is that guilt I see on his snubbed-nosed features?* She sat up straighter on the satin pillow that her human, Jenny, had so thoughtfully put out for her. *Is monsieur hiding something from me?*

Jake waddled in a circle before lying down, ignoring the suspicious look Princess was giving him. *Yes, dammit, I have her bone. If she thinks I'm giving it back, the chick's got another think coming.* He released a long, snorty breath and folded his paws over the huge bone he'd dug up on her side of the tree.

The pooch wouldn't be half bad looking if she'd do something with that kinky hair. That particular shade of white was becoming on her—and those bows. Hot damn. She was a classy canine.

Princess settled down, daintily licking a paw, casting looks in his direction. *Jake. What a manly name. When my human, Jenny, tied me beside him a couple of months ago, I thought he was nothing but an uncouth ruffian. But now he's starting to communicate with me. Brash though his snorts and licks might be, it was still communication. If it wasn't for that snotty nose and wrinkled face, he'd be—interesting. Oui! What a seductive waddle. Talk about buns of steel.*

As Jake continued to ignore her, Princess barked.

At the sound of her squeaky voice, Jake sprang to his feet and turned in a dizzying circle. That did it. The dame was gettin' to him. Show her an ounce of kindness and now she wouldn't keep quiet. "Will you shut up! I'm trying to sleep!"

Princess batted her eyes sweetly. "How utterly boorish, monsieur! You shouldn't be sleeping in the middle of the afternoon. You're supposed to be guarding your human's kite shop!''

Jake turned his back to her. The prissy canine was really steppin' on his bad side.

''Listen, Frenchie, the name's Jake, not that 'man sewer' you keep calling me.''

Princess yipped again and twirled on her hind legs. ''You lazy *bouledogue!* Sleeping in the middle of the afternoon!''

Jake lifted an eyelid to watch her. Holy Moly. Who'd she think she was? A circus performer? ''Mind your own business, lap rat. It is *not* my job to watch the kite shop. I'm here because my human can't leave me at home.'' He snorted. ''Says I disturb the neighbors.''

Princess daintily paused. ''I can understand that. You're disturbing me.''

Yawning, he refused to rise to her bait. ''Disturbing what? Yipping? That's your job? Yipping?''

She trotted over to get in his face. ''No, my job is nipping.'' She clamped her teeth hard on his ear.

''Ow!'' *Blood.* ''Is that blood?'' Jake bounded to his feet and crouched in a fighting stance.

One well-placed bat with a mean right paw, and she flipped head over heels to the end of her chain.

She let out a squall that would wake the dead.

What a pansy, he thought as she rolled over on her back, stuck both paws in the air and let out the most unconvincing whine he'd ever heard.

He jammed his paw on her stomach. ''Be quiet!'' His eyes anxiously darted to the candy store. ''You're gonna have the humans on us.''

"RIGHT." Dave Kasada shifted the phone to his other ear, trying to keep an eye on his bulldog through the front window. "Don't worry about it, Stu. I'll stay on the island a few more weeks to make sure the new line is off to a good start." He frowned when he saw Jenny McNeill's poodle, Princess, strut around Jake like a queen holding court. The dogs had been at each other for weeks, and the way Jenny pampered her mutt didn't help the matter. Until that poodle came, Jake hadn't given him a minute's trouble. The love-hate relationship between the two dogs was annoying. If Jenny McNeill would only keep her nose out of it, the pets would get along fine.

"No. I'm here, Stu. Just checking on my dog. The new line is our biggest seller to date. I should have put the Space Alien design into production months ago."

Kite flying was a growing pastime all over the world. The modernistic designs created by his company were so popular that orders from Europe, East Asia, Korea, China and Thailand were coming in faster than Rockfield Corporation could fill them.

"The kids love them, the adults love them—hey! Dog!" he shouted, nearly bursting the eardrum of his vice president of manufacturing. "Get away! Not you, Stu. I'm talking to a poodle.

"Yeah, I'm losing it. Guess I miss Chicago more than I thought I would." That wasn't exactly true. Taking over the management of their prototype store had been a catharsis for him. Fighting his ex-wife for visitation rights with his six-year-old daughter, Megan, had worn him down. The past few weeks experiencing Mackinac Island's easy pace gave him a breather from his problems. Even with the steady flow of tourists, he enjoyed the laid-back, peaceful atmosphere. Lately, the starry nights and sparkling waters of Mackinac Straits had made him long for female companionship. A moonlight carriage ride with a beautiful woman was beginning to sound good—an unusual thought for him. He'd sworn off women.

"As I was saying, a few more weeks—maybe until early fall. I'm staying in Aunt Mosie's house—she insists I'll be more comfortable there than at one of the hotels. Yeah, hip replacement. She's staying with her daughter, Carol, in Detroit."

He wasn't in any hurry to leave Mackinac Island. Mackinac weather was nice this time of year. The two-mile-wide, three-mile-long island covered two thousand two hundred acres and saw close to a million visitors annually. On long sunny days, a teenager worked in the kite shop while he played one of the three golf courses on the island—preferably the Wawashkamo, the one remaining links course in the United States.

Winter presented problems he didn't want to deal with. Weather permitting, the ferries ran until the second of January. After that, transportation to and from the island was by plane, but he didn't intend to worry about that. By then the fudge shop's lease would be up, and he could take over the space to enlarge the kite shop.

"Go full throttle with the expansion plans. We'll need two new production lines to handle the Martian and three for the Visitor— Hey! Get away!'' he yelled.

"Sorry, the damn poodle is annoying Jake again.

"Yes, getting rid of that dog is another advantage of taking over the Fudgeballs floor space.

"Hell, no, McNeill doesn't know.''

Jenny McNeill didn't have any inkling he was the head of Rockfield Corporation, the organization that owned the building. He didn't want her running to him every five minutes about a faulty water heater or a leaky roof. He paid others to do that. He wanted to concentrate on his designs.

Not that he felt good about what he was about to do. Putting a tenant out on the street wasn't his usual modus operandi, but now that the kite store had proven profitable and was an excellent test market for new products, he was hurting for space. An enterprising young woman like McNeill wouldn't have any trouble finding new quarters.

"Don't sweat it, Stu. I *am* Rockfield. I'll take the flak if we move too fast. The kites are a sure hit.

"Don't worry about McNeill. I'll have her out of the fudge shop in sixty days, max.

"Right. Call if you need me.''

He hung up, then dialed Freeman Investigation and asked for Sam Freeman. Freeman might be a nutcase, but a better investigator couldn't be found. "Sam? Dave Kasada. Have you found my ex-wife yet?''

The colorful, retired police officer spoke in a clipped, monotone voice. "Sorry, Mr. Kasada. I've tracked her to Paris, but the trail's cooled. Seems she and your daughter spent a few days doing the tourist scene, then disappeared.''

Dave muttered an expletive. ''August is my month to have Megan. It's July, and I haven't heard a word from Nancy all summer. Nancy can't just up and run off with her! What's a six-year-old kid doing in Europe? Dammit, find her! That's what I'm paying you for!''

''Give it another week. I have a source who says they've been spotted in Nice. I'll check it out,'' Sam said.

Nice. *Nice!* Nancy knew exactly where to hit him to make it hurt. The woman was cold, selfish, thoughtless as hell. Off to Nice without a word. What had he been thinking when he married her? He'd been taken with her body instead of her brains, Dave reflected, but he'd imagined he'd loved her. Eight years later he knew he never had. Nancy had never loved him, either. But once Rockfield Corporation began making a lot of money, Nancy had done a great job as a corporate wife. She'd been good at entertaining and charming investors and bankers. She had pushed to expand Rockfield, but he had resisted. Dave didn't want to be CEO of a huge conglomerate with no time to see his family. That's when Nancy had asked for a divorce—and taken Megan with her. The best thing that came from the marriage was Megan. He'd move heaven and earth to get her back.

He'd petitioned the court for full custody of his daughter, but Nancy came from a long line of attorneys. He had enough money to fight her writs and petitions but soon realized it was pointless. He wasn't about to drag his daughter through the courts. After considerable legal wrangling, he'd been granted one full summer month of custody. August was his month, so where was Megan? In Europe somewhere. The past year had been divorce hell, and Nancy's latest power play made his blood boil.

He banged the receiver down and looked out the window. The rich aroma of fudge drifted through the open doorway. A long line of tourists blocked the kite shop entrance as they waited to buy fudge. There were enough sugar fixes on the island to kill a normal tourist, but there they stood, elbow to elbow in front of Fudgeballs, obstructing his doorway, running off his business. He pitched a ball of string on the counter and disappeared to the back room.

DURING A LULL in business, Jenny McNeill glanced up from the batch of maple fudge she was stirring. She frowned when she heard Princess squeal.

"Darn that bulldog!" Tossing the wooden spoon aside, she marched out the front door, snatched up the poodle and brushed dirt off her snow-white underbelly. "What's wrong, sweetie? Is that pesky bulldog bothering you again?"

Princess whined, gazing at her.

Jenny glared at Jake. "Shoo—get away!"

Jake planted his stocky body and fixed his gaze on her. *That's my blood on the poodle's mouth, lady. Check it out. Ever heard of DNA?*

"Shoo! Get away, get. Bad dog!"

The door to Flying High burst open and Dave

stepped out. "I heard that! Jake wasn't doing a thing to Princess!"

Jenny cradled the miniature poodle protectively to her breast. "Mr. Kasada, this is the third time this week Jake has jumped poor, defenseless Princess."

Defenseless? Jake wanted to shout. *Ever seen* Jaws, *lady? With those choppers, your poor, defenseless Princess could have played the leading role!* He sat on his haunches beside his human. Dave would handle this.

"I was watching the whole thing out the front window." Dave crossed his arms and stared at her. "Your poodle was the instigator. She bit Jake on the ear."

Jenny's mouth fell open. "Princess would *never* bite without provocation!"

Just because Dave Kasada bore an uncanny resemblance to Kevin Costner, he wasn't going to intimidate her. She tucked a lock of hair behind her ear, wondering if he noticed she needed a touch-up. Her honey blond had faded to a mousy brown. She hadn't had time for a color in weeks. "Why don't you keep your bully home?"

Her neighbor glared at her through narrowed eyes. "You keep your prima donna home."

Stiffening, she counted to ten, determined to make the best of the situation. She hoped the man and his annoying bulldog would be gone soon, but there was no need to make the situation any more unpleasant than it already was. Hank Linstrom of Rockfield had told her Kasada would probably move out by fall. She hoped sooner. She desperately needed his space to expand Fudgeballs.

Dave had only opened Flying High for the summer, Linstrom had told her, as an experiment. Then he and his annoying dog would be gone.

"If you're not going to keep your dog locked up at home, then at least keep him away from mine." She cuddled her dog closer. "Princess is sensitive and not accustomed to your dog's ruffian behavior."

Dave uncrossed his arms. "I'll keep Jake home the day you take that paranoid poodle for therapy." He turned and walked into Flying High, slamming the door behind him.

"Well—well…" Jenny sputtered, unable to come up with a proper insult. The nerve of that jerk!

Kneeling, she carefully adjusted the small canopy shading Princess's pink cushion. "Please, baby, try to get along just a little longer." She glanced toward the kite shop. "That ill-tempered bulldog's days are numbered, I can assure you. There's only one tree here. You wouldn't want me to tie you out back in the hot sun, would you?"

Princess drew back as if she understood the threat and didn't like it.

Jenny shot another cross look at the kite store. Dave Kasada was the one who needed therapy, not Princess. The man had kites on the brain, plus he was antisocial. No wonder he didn't have the business she did. He probably scared every little kid who came into his shop. On the surface, he appeared perfectly normal, but he'd hung around Jake so long, he barked at people instead of talking. Women might find him attractive, but to her, he was as big a nuisance as his dog.

She patted Princess, glared at Jake, then ran inside to stir the boiling candy in the large copper kettle on the antique stove she had placed in the front window of her shop. Letting her prospective customers see her at work through the window was a marketing ploy that worked successfully. Indeed, Fudgeballs was a success—or it would be soon. Jenny had her good business sense and the unique flavoring she ordered from the orient made the candy unequaled.

All she needed now was that bank loan and Dave Kasada's space.

The phone rang and she snatched it up, waving her assistant, Rob Levitt, aside. She recognized her account executive's voice on the other end of the line.

"Yes, Mr. Snowden, everything is moving along nicely." Jenny hoped she sounded convincing enough. Actually, her business plans had stalled. With the tourist season in full swing, she hadn't had time to get a financial report together. Without the financial report there would be no loan, and without the loan, there would be no expansion.

"No, there's no problem. Mr. Linstrom at Rockfield has told me that when Mr. Kasada moves the kite shop space will be mine."

She swatted Rob's hand away from the cooling batch of fudgeballs. "No, Rockfield has always been easy to deal with. I've leased my side of the building for over five years. The kite shop just opened in May. He won't have trouble finding a new location for the kites—though he'll probably have to go to Mackinac City.''

Rockfield might support her expansion plans, but she wasn't sure Dave Kasada would. He'd undoubtedly be upset if he decided he wanted to stay, but business was business. Fudgeballs *would* expand.

''Of course, I'll have that report to you no later than next week.'' She smiled. ''Flying High should vacate the premises within sixty days—max.''

Reaching for a box of cocoa, she added, ''Have a nice day, Mr. Snowden... Mark. Of course, Mark. Please call me Jenny. Yes, I'll be talking to you soon.''

She hung up, sagging against the counter. ''Rob, I *have* to get that financial report together. Addison-Smyth Investments wants it on their desk yesterday.''

Rob smiled. The tall, spindly, twentyish-looking man with long black hair neatly pulled into a ponytail was never rattled. The round wire-rim glasses perched on the end of his nose gave him a boyish look. In the sixties he would have been called a love child. Jenny simply thought of him as her right hand.

''I can stay late tonight if you want.'' He carefully arranged spheres of warm, creamy chocolate in thin paper cups.

''Thanks. You're a trooper. I have to dig through the last five years of income tax records and show where my business has increased its profits.''

''Sounds like a lot of work.''

''It is.'' She paused, wondering how to broach the subject tactfully. ''I could have used Teensy's help this week.''

She was sympathetic to Rob's girlfriend, but Teensy *was* an employee. When Rob Levitt and Teensy Moffit came to her looking for work, they had assured her that being unmarried parents of an eight-month-old baby girl wouldn't be a problem. But that hadn't been the case. Teensy stayed home with baby Dory more often than she came to work.

Rob carried a large tray of fudge to the front case and began restocking. "The baby's been awful cranky lately—so has Teensy, for that matter."

Jenny's heart shot to her throat. "Rob? Teensy isn't..."

Rob glanced up. "Oh, no, she's not pregnant. I think she's homesick. She misses her family."

Jenny breathed a sigh of relief. Rob and Teensy were barely adults themselves. One child was enough.

"I'm serious, Jenny. I'll stay late if you want to work on that report this evening."

Jenny shook her head. "No, I can spare a couple of hours before I go to bed." She tasted the new batch of fudge.

"What happens when your loan's approved?" Rob closed the case and returned to a long marble table where vanilla-walnut fudge was cooling.

"We bump out the wall and double our square footage."

Rob frowned. "You think Mr. Kasada will just roll over and play dead? He might not want to leave the island. Space is so limited, and his kite shop seems to be doing a good business."

Standing on tiptoe, Jenny rummaged around on a shelf, looking for a box of salt. "Mr. Linstrom assured me Mr. Kasada will be no problem. He said that by fall Dave would probably be looking into relocating. Mackinac City is a good business area and just sixteen minutes from the island.''

''But the tourists love his kites—especially those alien things. Awesome, really rad.''

She measured two teaspoons of salt into a kettle. ''I don't mean to sound heartless, but I can't be worried about the kite shop.'' She glanced out the front window, frowning when she saw Jake slobbering on Princess. ''Relocating is Dave Kasada's problem.'' She ignored the sudden twinge of guilt. Relocating wouldn't be easy, and she didn't envy him the task. It was the last thing in the world she'd want to do.

''Rob, don't breathe a word to Dave about the expansion until the lease is signed. He might contact Rockfield and put a kink in my plans.''

Rob made a zipping motion across his mouth. ''If you don't need me to work late, maybe I'll take Teensy out to eat.'' He glanced at Jenny. ''If I can find someone to keep Dory—like I said, she's kind of fussy. Teensy gets all nervous if we leave her with someone she doesn't know.''

Jenny's hand paused over the kettle. ''Rob, is everything all right between you and Teensy?''

''Oh...yes, I guess so. I promised her we'd visit my folks in New York as soon as I can scrape up the money. They're anxious to see the baby.''

Jenny smiled when she thought of Dory. So beautiful, with her curly black hair, dark eyes and spiky black lashes. When she held the baby in her arms, she felt a strong maternal pull.

"You and Teensy need some time alone." Jenny couldn't believe what she was about to offer. She needed an eight-month-old to care for in addition to going through old tax records like she needed a gunshot wound to her head. "Drop Dory by my place tonight. I'll keep her for you."

"But your report—"

"I can work on it while I watch the baby. No problem." No problem? What was she thinking? "Dory's a doll. We get along great." She smiled. "Besides, maybe a night out is all Teensy needs to boost her spirits."

"Thanks." Another group of customers came in as Rob slid a tray of fudge onto the counter. "We'll bring the baby by early."

"Great." Jenny grinned. "She can run the calculator for me."

2

DAVE YANKED OPEN the door and yelled at Jake. "Knock it off! Both of you!" The dogs were at it again, barking and circling each other like prizefighters.

He closed the screen, snatched up a broom and started sweeping the front entrance.

"Hey, mister!" a kid called through the screen door.

He glanced up. "Yes?"

"How much is that Martian kite?"

"Eighteen ninety-five."

The kid's face fell. "Cool."

Damn right, cool. The kites were engineering genius. He softened when he saw the child's look of disappointment.

"Tell your folks I'm running a special today—nine ninety-eight."

The kid's face brightened. "Really!" He tore off down the street in search of his parents.

Dave felt a surge of elation followed by a twinge of conscience. He was damn proud of his kites. The business was exceeding his expectations. So why the guilt trip? Rockfield had owned the building that housed Flying High for twenty years. It was just never put to proper use. When his grandfather, Forte Kasada, handed the business down to him, he'd began to utilize all its assets. Expanding was his chance to bring Flying High into the nineties, to pump new ideas into the company. Grandpa had been a little skeptical—too old-fashioned, he swore—but he was thrilled by how well the kites had done.

When Dave opened the shop last May, he did so with the intent of expanding Flying High to twice its size and adding six to eight more test-marketing designs. It made him feel good to know Grandpa thought he made the right choice giving the business to him.

The Mothership was on the drawing board. Next month, LifeForms.

He glanced out the window, frowning when he saw the poodle lick Jake's ear and pin Jake against the tree. Just like a woman. Break a man down, then whine when he goes after her.

He swept a clump of dirt out the front door and closed it. Good business practice didn't make his job any easier, but the sooner he told McNeill her lease would not be renewed, the better it would be for all concerned.

At least he'd be rid of the annoying poodle.

PRINCESS LET OUT a pitiful yip. *Monsieur Bouledogue* refused to notice her! She'd danced and strutted, but the old jaw-jutted slug just laid there like a lump of coal.

She chanced a glance at the kite shop, then raised her yip a decibel.

Must be hard of hearing.

Another decibel.

Nothing. *There's definitely something wrong with him. Every male canine on the island makes advances, but not him.*

She leaped sideways, then executed a perfect back flip—her cutest trick.

Jake kept his eyes on an object between his paws.

What is he so preoccupied with? Looks like some old bone. Can't understand how a piece of carcass could be more appealing than moi. She eyed him resentfully. It just wasn't natural.

She returned to her pillow and glanced over her hindquarters. The problem must have something to do with his legs. They were seriously bowed. And his manly assets were almost dragging the ground. That had to be uncomfortable. Had he injured something on one of those amorous romps so essential to his manly libido? That must be it. No wonder he was such a grouch.

JAKE SNORTED, watching her flit back and forth. Didn't the dame ever calm down? She was acting like a flea on steroids, jumping around, doing back flips. *If she doesn't quit wiggling in my face, she's gonna get a lesson.* He smacked his lips. If only her human, Jenny, would take a hike.

He shoved the large bone under his belly, wondering if Princess had noticed it yet. Hell, he didn't even know if it was her bone, but he wasn't taking any chances. Had to be, though. It came from her side of the tree, so she could rightfully claim it.

His eyelids drooped shut, only to fly open at the sound of the bell hanging over the door of Fudgeballs.

Uh-oh. Human alert!

"Here you are, sweetums." Jenny held up a treat for the poodle. Princess dashed to her, sprang to her hind legs and hopped and twirled.

Jake covered his eyes with his paw. *Holy Moly, the stupid broad's gonna break her back.* He snorted and laid his head down. *As if a tiny snack is gonna excite me.*

When Jenny was out of earshot, Jake got up, walked to the poodle's side of the tree and watched for a moment while she daintily washed her paw with her tongue. "I wouldn't have acted *that* stupid over a T-bone steak."

Her head snapped up. "T-bone? *Bon chagrin!*" Her eyes widened. "You eat *beef?*"

"What the hell do you think I eat? Oats?" He snorted. "In case you haven't noticed, I'm a red-blooded dog. I eat meat."

She sighed, exasperated. "No *wonder* you look like you do, all wrinkled and puffy. The cholesterol—my heavens."

Puffy? No one had ever accused him of looking puffy. He lifted his gaze. "What do dancing poodles eat these days?"

"Chicken. Maybe a little fish."

Figures. He yawned, dropped to the ground and laid his head between his paws. "Must be why your hair looks like a Brillo pad."

Her back bristled and her tail shot straight up, wagging back and forth irritably. In three hops she was on him, tearing into his good ear.

"Ow, ow, ow, ow!" Jake swatted at her, but he didn't want to use his full strength in case he hurt the silly poodle.

Princess calmly strutted to her canopy and sat down as Jenny burst out the door.

Jake waddled to his side of the tree, lying on his left ear to soothe it. Then he rolled onto his back and howled for mercy.

Princess snuggled against Jenny's leg, darting smirking looks at Jake. "Yip, yip, yip!" *Shut up! I didn't even draw blood this time, you big bébé.*

Jake trotted toward her, skidding to a stop when he saw Jenny grab the hose and turn on the outside faucet. Before he had a chance to say woof, a blast of cold water hit him in the face.

Yikes! Howling, he bolted for safety. *What's with this human? Is she nuts? Hey, I'm the injured party here!*

DAVE KASADA stood in the doorway of the kite shop, staring at the scene in front of him.

"Don't turn that on my dog."

"Your dog bit Princess!"

"Bit her? Was Jake—"

"Being amorous? Hardly." Jenny tightened her lips, determined to hide her exasperation.

"Put that hose away." Dave walked to the tree, leaned down and patted Jake. "The women giving you a bad time, sport?"

Jake snorted.

"Your dog is not a sport." Jenny pointed at Jake. "He keeps Princess in a constant state of turmoil."

"Really." Dave crossed his arms. "Could it be that Princess is neurotic? Jake gets along with other dogs."

Jenny pitched the hose aside and turned off the faucet. "I don't have time to argue. Just keep your dog away from mine." She attempted to go into the fudge shop, but he blocked her entrance.

"Jenny—it is Jenny, isn't it?"

"Look, Mr. Kasada—" She pushed a lock of hair out of her eye. Even though he'd been in the shop on occasion, mostly to play with Dory, they had barely spoken. She was always too busy to visit, and he seemed more interested in the baby than her.

He shoved his hands into the front pockets of his pants. "Call me Dave."

"Dave." A red flag went up. That would be stupid. Much better to keep the relationship impersonal. When he was loading his belongings into a truck, personal sentiments could get in the way.

She studied his intimidating six-foot frame. He always wore perfectly pressed Dockers, usually with a Polo shirt, and gave the appearance he'd be more comfortable on a golf course than in a kite shop. He looked good from the top of his well-groomed blond head to his expensive Italian shoes. She laughed. What was a man like him doing with a bulldog and working in a kite shop?

"Listen. I'm behind in my work. I can't be constantly running out here to break up the dogs. Just do me a favor and keep Jake out of the way—or better yet, in the store with you.''

He kicked the end of the hose out of his way. "You keep your dog in your store.''

She pretended his good looks didn't affect her. Under different circumstances, she'd die to catch his eye. But liking Dave meant liking his dog, and the bulldog drove her nuts.

"I can't have an animal in the shop. I serve food. Why can't you keep your dog in *your* shop?''

Dave laughed. "Jake in a kite shop? That's a good one. Jake's docile, but he's clumsy as hell.''

No kidding, she thought.

"He could tear up a couple dozen kites without trying.''

"Well, something has to be done. I'm shorthanded, and I can't run out here every five minutes. I have a special order for twelve dozen fudgeballs wrapped in gold foil and tied with white silk ribbons to be delivered to the Grand Hotel by four o'clock this afternoon, in addition to waiting on my walk-in customers.''

His look turned chilly. "Then you don't have time to stand here discussing dogs.''

"You're right. I don't.'' They stared at each other.

He glanced through her open door. "Where's your help?''

"Rob's here. Teensy didn't come in today.''

Why was she standing here telling him her life's history when she should be starting another batch of fudge? The reason for her delay wasn't hard to define. It was nice to have a conversation with someone whose every other word wasn't "man" or "awesome." Rob's and Teensy's conversations went, "That's awesome, man." Or on occasion, "Man, ain't that awesome?"

For some reason he wasn't rushing off, either. "I've missed seeing their baby around lately. She's cute, isn't she?"

"Dory's a doll—I really have to go. Teensy hasn't been in a lot, and Rob seems preoccupied recently—look, Mr. Kasada—"

"Dave."

"Dave." She smiled, aware that his hazel eyes had softened. Cripes. It wouldn't hurt to be civil. "I really have to get back to work."

They stared at each other until Jenny looked at the dogs. Jake waddled to his side of the tree and hiked his leg, eyeing Princess. She stuck her nose in the air and returned to her cushion, curling herself into a fetal position.

Dave strolled to the sidewalk with her. "I don't mean to sound presumptuous, but your business seems to be going great guns lately."

Pride assailed her, thrilled that he would notice how well Fudgeballs was doing.

"It is, thank you." He opened the door and she went inside. He followed. "More than I had anticipated. I'm afraid I should have hired additional help when it was available."

"Yes...there's not too many part-timers looking for work right now." Dave cleared his throat. "I'm lucky to have Peter Nelson working for me four hours a day." He studied the small quarters. "Your space is really limited. If you hired more help, wouldn't they be walking over each other?''

She caught her breath. He could see she desperately needed more space. Did he know what he was implying? No, he couldn't. He was just making small talk without the slightest inkling she intended to get more space—his space. Guilt flooded her, but she shoved it aside. It wasn't exactly her fault the kite shop couldn't stay. It was up to Rockfield Corporation. She was such a long-time tenant, they would agree to her expansion.

He ambled to a table piled with taffy. ''Looks to me like you need a couple thousand more feet.''

She avoided his eyes. ''Boy, do I.''

When he laughed, she realized it was a wonderful sound. Not loud, not soft, very masculine. *Dang it. Stop it. Next we'll be inviting each other over for coffee.*

He stood back, his gaze casually spanning the room. ''Ever thought about getting a bigger place?''

She kept her head down, wrapping pieces of fudge. ''I've sort of had it in the back of my mind lately.'' Sort of? That's all she'd thought about. She couldn't believe he was making it easy for her.

''I've been thinking about expanding the kite shop.'' He left the table of taffy to peruse the trays of fudge in the display counter.

''Really?'' Her pulse jumped. Then he would be comfortable with his forced relocation. Mr. Linstrom hadn't conveyed Kasada's feelings on the matter, and it really was none of her business how he felt. She had to do what was best for Fudgeballs.

"That's great. I guess the kites are going so well you'll need a bigger place?" She recalled the various sizes and designs she'd seen in the window. Paper kites, plastic, shiny foil—in all shapes and forms.

He nodded. "You can't imagine how much space I need."

She smiled broadly. "Oh, but I can. You have so many sizes." She tried not to sound overly encouraging, but it was hard to hold back her enthusiasm.

"You ever been inside the shop?"

She shook her head.

"Got a spare minute?"

She didn't have a spare second, but she found herself wiping her hands on her apron and trailing him next door. She studied the way his slacks fit his tight little behind, and thoughts of Kevin Costner in *Tin Cup* blinded her. Nice. Very nice.

Inside the kite shop, she looked around and felt like a kid in Disney World. Colorful designs filled the store, hanging from the ceiling and walls, creating a fantasy world.

"You like kites?"

"Sure, who doesn't?" She inspected a vivid blue one and imagined it soaring into the sky, dancing among fluffy white clouds. "This one looks like fun."

He came over to stand behind her. She was surprised at her reaction to his masculinity. The smell of Polo floated lightly between them.

"That's the simplest design—flat diamond shape formed by two sticks tied into a cross. Then there's the box kite, open frame, rectangular."

"What are those that have no frame at all?"

"Parafoil."

"How do they fly?"

"The wind shapes them. See the triangular fins on the tail? They act as stabilizers."

Jenny picked up a vivid yellow hexagonal kite which, according to the tag, was called a three-sticker Malay. "I'm surprised to see there's such a demand for kites."

He smiled, and her pulse thumped like a schoolgirl's. He was in his world now. She marveled that his manly features held a boy's excitement. But he was no boy, and that's what bothered her.

"Fortunately, it's getting more and more popular as a sport—really big in Thailand."

"You're kidding." She knew that remark sounded silly, but she suddenly felt tongue-tied as he stepped closer.

"No, I'm serious. The all-Thailand championships are held in Bangkok every spring."

"You ship kites all the way to Thailand?"

"Ship them, buy from them—sort of a trade-off." He reached for the blue kite she favored. "This particular design comes from India. In India the kite string is coated with ground glass. The object is to cut the opponent's string."

She winced. "Sounds dangerous."

"In South America, the kite frames are armed with razor blades. Our competitions are tame in comparison."

"I can't imagine kite flying as a combat sport." Jenny smiled. "It was always just a pleasurable way to spend an afternoon when I was a kid—except when the kite got caught in a tree.''

He smiled again and their gazes caught. ''That happens a lot.''

His voice dropped to a low pitch. There was something...sensual about it. Straightening, she realized she'd stayed too long. She suddenly wanted to take the day off. Go on a picnic, eat ice cream, fly a kite.

''Definitely sounds like you need a place twice the size of this,'' she conceded.

''I'm glad you understand,'' he returned quietly.

What's to understand? He needs more space, I need more space—when he moves we'll both have what we want.

''I need to get back to my fudge kettle.'' She set a kite aside. ''The next set of tourists will invade us any moment.''

''Sorry to have bent your ear so long. I'm afraid I get carried away about my kites.''

And she'd gotten carried away with him. He'd spurred thoughts she shouldn't have. When he visited her shop, she felt secure, but in his shop it seemed too...too personal. ''There's something to say about loving your work.''

''I've monopolized the conversation,'' he apologized. He walked her to the door. ''Sometime I'd love to hear about—fudgeballs.'' He handed her the blue kite. ''For when you get a little spare time.''

''Thank you.'' She was touched by the gesture.

He opened the door. ''How do you keep that trim figure with all that candy around?''

The compliment nearly bowled her over. How long

had it been since a man noticed her figure? Too long—way too long. "The secret is to eat all you want—just don't swallow."

Her cheeks burned as she walked to her shop, knowing he watched her every step. She hoped he hadn't seen her blush.

"BROTHER! You see that, lap rat?" Jake strutted to Princess's side of the tree.

"*Pardon moi, monsieur.* Are you speaking to me?"

"Okay, okay. Did you see that, *Princess?*"

Princess sprang to her feet. "You mean how moony-eyed your human looked at my human?"

Jake snorted. "I mean the way *your* human looked at *my* human."

Princess wiggled closer and batted her lashes. "You mean like this?" She nuzzled her nose against his ear.

Jake felt the fur rise on his back. "Now cut that out! I don't need the hose thing again."

Shoot, she even smells good.

"You are so big and strong." She laid her head against his.

He swelled with pride and smacked his tongue over his nose. "Stick with me, baby, and we'll go places."

Princess yawned and curled up against his belly. Her eyes closed, then flew open. "How am I supposed to sleep with you so close?"

"Who said we were going to sleep?"

"ROB? I need more walnuts!" Jenny reached for a measuring cup. Rob didn't answer, and she called again. "Rob?"

Where was he? The vanilla was running low, and the front case had less than a dozen fudgeballs left. He should be starting new batches of both.

She walked to the back room, opened the pantry and stood with her hands on her hips, trying to decide how she was going to haul a hundred-pound bag of sugar to the front of the store.

Somebody sighed loudly, and she whirled to see Rob sitting on a crate of corn syrup, playing an electronic hand-held game of gin rummy. Baby Dory was next to him in her carrier, gurgling, her tiny hands happily flailing the air.

"Rob?" She hoped she sounded as exasperated as she felt. Teensy knew better than to ask Rob to take care of the baby on such a busy day. "What are you doing sitting back here playing gin rummy?"

Rob sighed. "It's heavy, boss lady."

His jaw quivered, his eyes red behind the wire-rimmed glasses. "What's heavy?" she asked, afraid of his answer.

"The mood scene. I need to chill a few minutes."

"Can you chill over the copper kettle? There's a tour group two blocks down the street. They'll be coming into the store any minute." Jenny leaned over and tickled Dory's stomach, producing a big, toothless grin. "Hi, sweetie."

Rob glumly hit the play button and watched the cards spin. "Teensy's split."

Jenny frowned. "Split what?"

He shrugged. "Left. Didn't say where, just dropped

Dory off and said I had to watch her until she got back.''

"When's she coming back?"

Rob shrugged again. "She didn't know. Maybe never." He looked as if he'd been kicked by a Clydesdale.

The announcement didn't surprise her. Teensy had been edgy and restless lately, but Jenny would never have dreamed the girl would run off and leave Dory behind.

"Why now? Was she that unhappy?"

"I don't know. She said she wants to travel, have fun like we used to. She wants to hang out and not work."

"Who doesn't?" Kneeling beside the crate, Jenny patted his arm wishing she felt more sympathetic, but she had a business to run. One more crisis to deal with. "I'm sorry. Is there anything I can do?"

Rob shook his head.

"I'll take Dory up front with me."

The indifferent rise and fall of shoulders said, "Whatever." He obviously needed time alone as badly as she needed vanilla and chocolate fudge, but she wasn't insensitive to his pain. Teensy was his anchor. Without her he was lost.

Jenny scooped up the baby carrier and took Dory to the front as the door of the shop opened. A group of Japanese tourists poured into the room.

"A pound of vanilla, please!"

"Two slices of maple nut!"

"Two dozens fudgeballs. Ma'am! Do you ship?"

Jenny rushed to fill orders, sneaking frantic glances

toward the back room. She could hear the electronic beep as the gin rummy wheels spun. Dory, confused by the noise and activity, started to fuss.

As Jenny moved between the register and the glass cases, she poked a pacifier into the baby's mouth. Her gaze strayed to the empty kettles, and the headache creeping up the back of her neck tightened. How long did it take to chill out? The candy supply would only last another few minutes.

The bell over the door tinkled, and a group of retired librarians crowded into the shop. A spindly matron started stuffing saltwater taffy into a bag as if it was going out of style.

Dory let out a wail, her fists punching the air to emphasize it was a half hour past lunchtime.

Making change for a twenty, Jenny strained to hear a customer's remarks above the baby's squalling, then leaned over and thrust the pacifier into Dory's mouth.

The phone shrilled.

She grabbed it up. "Fudgeballs." She listened, her heart sinking. "Of course, six dozen isn't out of the question—I only wish you'd called earlier—no, I can have them. Yes, I'll be there no later than four." She hung up. The special order she'd told Dave about now included an additional six dozen fudgeballs—six dozen she didn't have.

Rob appeared in the doorway, the gin rummy game dangling loosely in his right hand. He looked as if he'd walked through a mine field. "Like, need some help?"

Like, does a victim of the Sahara Desert need a fan? Jenny nodded, her eyes gesturing to the dwindling fudge supply. "Can you start a batch of chocolate?"

Rob moseyed to the copper kettle and began dumping in ingredients. Jenny prayed his mind was on work and not on his stormy love life.

It was two o'clock before the rush eased off. "Dory is starving—and soaking wet." Jenny stripped off her apron. "You want to take her in the back and change her?"

Pouring chocolate fudge onto the marble table, Rob didn't answer. Apparently, he was still chilling, but at least he was working during the process.

"Better yet, why don't *I* take her in the back and change her," Jenny said to herself. The wedding party wouldn't mind if their fudgeballs arrived after the reception was over.

By the time she had the baby changed and the jars of mixed vegetables and fruit dessert warmed, Dory was screaming at the top of her lungs. Sweat formed on Jenny's upper lip as she spooned pureed vegetables into the baby's mouth, realizing if Rob didn't pull out of his funk soon, she would have full responsibility of the child. Taking care of an angel like Dory would be fun on most days, but not today.

Teensy's timing couldn't be worse. The financial report lay on Jenny's desk, untouched. She was due at the Grand Hotel in less than two hours to set up for the wedding. Rob had to watch the shop or she'd have to close—unthinkable this time of the year.

She spooned the last of the fruit dessert into Dory's mouth and wiped the baby's face, then removed her bib and carried her to the front. Rob was working on the six dozen fudgeballs for the reception.

"Are we going to make it?" Jenny sat the baby on the counter.

Nodding, Rob sighed and fashioned another chocolaty sphere.

"Yum." Jenny made a playful face at Dory. "Warm chocolate—want a bite?" She pinched a tiny corner off and tasted it, frowning as she spat it out in a napkin.

Rob glanced up questioningly.

"You put salt in the candy instead of sugar!"

His face fell. "Bummer."

"Bummer" was putting it mildly. They had less than two hours to produce the candy for the wedding. In Rob's present state, it was impossible. She handed the baby to him, then moved him aside.

Barking orders, she reached for the measuring cups. "Wait on customers while I make the candy. If it gets too busy, step next door and ask Dave if he'd mind helping out." He'd been so understanding this morning, she felt she could take such liberties. She'd do the same for him.

Space wasn't the main problem here now—it was Rob, and if she didn't get some help she was going to pull her hair out.

AT EXACTLY THREE FIFTY-NINE, Jenny pedaled past the front of the Grand Hotel, which glimmered like a diamond on an island of brilliant green. Tourists who had indulged in midafternoon high tea were leaving, some taking the horse-drawn carriages lining the drive. She wished she had time for a romantic carriage ride herself, but romance didn't go very far when you were alone.

Jenny stopped her bicycle by the side entrance, set the kickstand, then picked up the two boxes that held her neatly stacked fudgeballs, all tied in pretty white and gold ribbons, from the cart behind the back wheel. She'd only taken a few steps when a shot of water from an in-ground sprinkler caught her foot and soaked it.

She opened the metal door and started down the plush carpeted hall of the hotel toward the banquet room. The sucking sound of her wet sneakered foot resounded like a belch in church. When an elderly couple passed her, they stared and shook their heads as she squeaked and squished past them.

Was it the obnoxious sound of her shoe or her lack of proper attire? She wasn't dressed for high tea or a wedding. She should have changed from shorts to a dress. She adjusted the boxes in her arms to pull the brass handle on the door. The moment she stepped inside, her breath caught in her throat.

The fragrance of gardenias and sweet peas permeated the air around her. Beautiful bouquets graced each round table, set with fine china and crystal glassware. The bride had given thought to every detail of the reception, just as Jenny would if it was her wedding.

She took a few more soggy steps before the hotel attendants stopped arranging an elaborate display of fruit and cheeses to stare at her. "I'm here to deliver the fudgeballs the bride requested. I'll stay out of your way,'' she said, trying to make herself inconspicuous as she approached the elaborately decorated podium where the wedding party was to be seated.

After distributing the first two boxes of fudgeballs, one neatly tied pack set to the left of each place card, she returned to her cart outside for the next load. As she walked into the hotel, thoughts of her own wedding filled her mind.

She had fantasized about a reception similar to this one, but Brian had never gotten around to popping the all-important question. Instead, he'd hint about getting married, leading her to false hopes and dreams. With each fudgeball she placed on the wedding tables, thoughts of what could have been ran through her mind.

The set-up took longer than she expected, and it was past five-thirty. She pushed open the door with her free hand and walked toward the cart at the back of her bike. She paused to look at the water and sighed. Sore muscles reminded her she hadn't worked out lately, and the pit of her stomach confirmed she'd skipped lunch. Her legs felt weak, and her head relayed a light, dizzy feeling.

''Need a hand?''

She glanced up to see Dave peddling toward her. He parked his bike, then stepped toward her and took the empty boxes from her hand, his skin brushing hers. The scent of his cologne tickled her senses more than the flowers in the reception hall.

''Thanks,'' was all she could mumble as she watched him stack the empty boxes in the cart. He presented the nicest view from behind.... She mentally shook herself. She must be more light-headed than she thought. Mr. Kite Man was off-limits, no matter how he filled out his Dockers. "What brings you to this side of the island?"

"I had to mail my daughter's birthday present. She'll be seven on Thursday."

She laughed. "Taking the long way home?" The post office was closer to their shops than to the hotel.

"I need the exercise. I've stood behind the counter most of the day."

"What about your helper?"

"He didn't show up today."

"Odd," she said, laughing. "We're both having trouble keeping help."

"Oh?"

"Teensy's flown the coop. Rob's devastated. Not much help."

"Left the island? I thought I heard the baby crying earlier."

"You did. Rob's trying to work and take care of Dory, in addition to pining over Teensy."

They climbed on their bikes and pedaled off side by side. Jenny glanced at him. "You have a daughter? I didn't realize you're married."

"Was," he corrected.

The bitterness in his voice shocked her. "I'm sorry."

"Don't be. Not having my daughter with me is my only regret about my divorce."

They pedaled along the shoreline drive where the water lay like a blue jewel in the hot sun.

"Does your daughter live nearby?"

His laugh was anything but amused. "No. She lives in Chicago, but her mother's taken her to Europe for the summer."

"That's nice."

"Nice," he corrected. "She's in Nice," he explained. "I'm trying to track her down. I'm supposed to have my daughter come stay with me next month, but Nancy disappeared a couple of weeks ago with her. I had to mail Megan's birthday present to Chicago. God only knows how long it will be before she gets it."

The hostility in his voice had changed to vulnerability. Jenny realized he was hurting. The attention he showered on Dory suddenly made sense. He missed his daughter, so much so he tried to appease his loneliness through another child.

For the first time, she felt at peace with her decision to end her relationship with Brian. She was still plagued by an occasional doubt, but hearing Dave's problems strengthened her belief that she'd made the right choice. She and Brian had the right chemistry but the wrong formula for a lasting relationship. Unlike Brian, she'd have no problem committing to marriage and babies, but when she did, she wanted it to last.

Forever.

3

"HEADS UP, FRENCHIE!" Jake nudged the sleeping Princess with his hip. "Something's happening—it don't look right."

Princess fluttered her eyelashes and focused on Rob lifting Dory from the baby carrier of his bicycle. The morning sun glistened off the Mackinac Straits.

"Uh-oh, Jenny's not going to like him bringing the baby to work again." Princess yawned. "Why's he so early?"

"Check it out, sleepyhead. He ain't coming to work." Jake snorted and licked his nose. "Look's like everything he owns is packed in that bag on the bike."

Princess rose and strutted to the end of her chain, straining to get a good look at the cycle. She hurried toward Rob and sniffed his shoes, then turned to Jake, who had joined her. "He's wearing clean socks," Princess whispered.

Jake snorted. "I'd say he's flying the coop. Why else would he be wearing socks at all?"

Princess started leaping in circles. "Oh, no, oh, no! He *can't* leave. Jenny needs him." She jumped and barked at Rob.

Jake swatted her with his paw. "Get a grip, curly locks. Get a grip."

Princess sat down, then jumped up again. "And the baby—what would we do without the baby?"

"Will you calm down? You'll get yourself all lathered up—and you know what that does to that kinky hair of yours."

They both sat as quiet as church mice while Rob laid the carryall on the fudge shop's doorstep, kissed Dory on the forehead, gave her a gentle pat, then turned, walked to his bicycle and rode away.

Jake yawned. "Looks like you're not going to have to worry about what to do *without* the baby—more like what're you gonna do *with* it."

A tiny whimper escaped Princess and she leaned into Jake. "Dory is so cute. Come, monsieur. We must say hello."

Jake waddled beside Princess, and the two peered inside the carrier. Sniff, sniff.

"What's that smell?" Jake asked.

"Baby powder. Isn't it exquisite!"

Jake burrowed his nose deeper to investigate a sputtering sound. He jumped back, snorted and shook from head to tail. "Phew! That ain't baby powder! That stinks. What'd she step in?"

Princess spun in a circle. "She doesn't walk, silly. She just did what comes natural to a baby. She dirtied her diaper."

"Dirtied? Hell, it smells like a pile of.... She's sitting in that?"

Princess ignored him, knowing she needed her human. "Yip, yip!" *Oh, Jenny! The baby needs changing.*

"Woof!" *Stay back, Dave! Run for your life!*

"Princess?" Jenny opened the screen door to look out. "Is that irritating bulldog—" Her gaze dropped to the step.

Baby Dory rubbed her eyes, blinking sleepily. When she saw Jenny, she burst into gurgling glee.

Dave stepped out of the kite shop, broom in hand. He glanced at the dogs, then at Jenny. "I've been keeping my eye on Jake. He hasn't done—" His gaze moved to Dory. "What's this?"

"I don't know. I came in early this morning, and Rob wasn't here." Jenny stooped to pick up the baby, frowning. She nuzzled Dory's neck and made the baby laugh. "Smells like you left a little present in your diaper."

Present? Jake rolled over and played dead.

Dave reached for the envelope pinned to the baby's jumper. "It's addressed to you."

Still frowning, Jenny handed Dory to Dave. She heard his sharp intake of breath as he quickly held the infant at arm's length, turning his face upwind.

Jenny read the letter, sinking to the wooden step. "He's gone," she whispered.

"Who?"

"Rob."

"Gone? Where?"

Jenny opened the letter and read aloud. "I'm sorry, Jenny, but I'm going after Teensy. My life is nothing without her. I know you will take good care of Dory.

Sorry to leave you in a bind, but you know how she hates to stay with strangers. Rob.''

"Hell." Dave assessed the situation. "You'll have to notify the authorities."

Jenny shot off the step. "That's the *last* thing I'd do."

"The child is abandoned—you can't just *keep* her."

"I can't report Dory abandoned! Rob's simply asked me to take care of her until he gets back." Heat suffused her cheeks. Turn Dory over to strangers? How insensitive could he be? "If I report Rob's actions to child services, they'll put her in foster care. I can't do that."

"Jenny, be reasonable." Dave shifted Dory in his arms. "Rob and Teensy are nothing but kids themselves—irresponsible ones at that. They've deserted their child!"

She brushed his arguments aside. How she handled the matter was none of his business. "You don't know anything about them. They love Dory. They'll be back."

"When does the note say they'll be back?"

"It doesn't—but I know Rob. He's upset right now, not thinking clearly. He may be young, but he's not irresponsible." She looked at Dory, wondering how she would manage until Rob found Teensy and convinced her to stay with him.

"And if they don't come back?"

"I'll take care of her, if that's what it takes."

"You?" He laughed. "What do you know about babies?"

Her chin lifted with resolve. She knew zilch about babies, but she couldn't let Rob down. He and Teensy would come to their senses and be back within the week. "Enough," she said.

Their gazes locked.

"Who'll run your business? You couldn't keep up with its demands even when Rob was helping you," he said.

She heard the phone ring and turned to answer it.

"Wait a minute! We're having a conversation!" Dave caught the door with his elbow and followed her in, still holding Dory a safe distance in front of him. The baby kicked and flailed her arms playfully. "Kid, you're potent," he grumbled.

Jenny answered the phone, glad to have a moment to try to pull together her thoughts. How *was* she going to manage?

Dave wrinkled his nose, whispering, "What should I do with her?"

Jenny waved him off, listening intently to the conversation and scribbling numbers on a pad. "Yes, yes, I can meet the deadline. No problem. Floridian blue ribbons, yes. Each box will have a blue ribbon. No, I won't forget. Yes, Floridian blue. Definitely Floridian. Yes, thank you for the order. No, I'll have them ready. No problem. Not navy blue, not pale blue, Floridian. I understand." Her hand trembled as she put the phone in the cradle.

"Big order?"

She stared into space. "What the heck is Floridian blue?"

Dave winced as Dory pulled the hairs on his arm. "What about the baby?"

Jenny snapped to attention. "Two days. I've got two days. Two hundred eighty-eight fudgeballs, two to a box—white box tied with blue ribbon. Make sure it's Floridian blue. Not navy blue, not pale blue. Floridian blue."

Dave swung Dory back and forth in front of Jenny's face. "In the meantime? What about the baby?"

"She needs to be changed."

"I *know* she needs to be changed. By now everyone on the island knows it."

Jenny grabbed the telephone book and rapidly thumbed through the pages. "I've got to find a replacement for Rob. I need help—desperately." She ran her index finger down a column of numbers.

Dave held Dory out to her again. "The baby?"

"Do you know anyone who needs a job?"

"I know someone who's *done* a job."

"Be serious."

"Take a whiff—you think this isn't serious?"

She settled on a number and punched it into the phone, cradling the receiver between her ear and her shoulder as she searched through a drawer, finally extracting a disposable diaper. "Here." She jammed the diaper under his chin. "Hello? Mrs. Wilcox? Jenny McNeill at the fudge shop. Could I interest you in a job?"

DAVE WET A CLOTH with warm water then stripped the soiled diaper off Dory. Memories flooded him as he wiped the tiny pink bottom. How many years had it been? He couldn't begin to count the number of times he'd changed Megan. She had been like Dory, playful and sweet. If only he could hold her again. Where was she? He could throttle Nancy!

"There we go, sweetie," he said, lifting Dory in his arms. She immediately stuck her thumb in her mouth and sucked loudly. "Hungry?" He bounced her on his shoulder and patted her back. "Let's see if we can find something."

He needed to get back to his shop, but when he looked at Dory, he softened. How could her parents abandon her? He'd do anything to have Megan with him.

"Did you find everything you needed?" Jenny asked, interrupting his thoughts.

"Everything except breakfast. I don't know how much longer her thumb will hold out."

Jenny smiled. "Isn't she cute?"

Jenny stood so close, her perfume intoxicated him. Chanel? "Yes, she's cute," he mused, thinking more in terms of Jenny herself. She was beautiful. He hadn't thought about a woman since his divorce, not seriously, so why did Jenny suddenly look and smell good to him? They could barely say two consecutive civil words to each other, and all of a sudden he was wondering if she'd go out to dinner if he asked. Her smile, the curve of her hip, long tan legs that tapered to trim ankles. Since when did ankles start looking so good? He'd been without female companionship too long.

"There's formula in the back room. Rob bought it

last week." Jenny wiped her hands on a towel. "I'll mix a bottle."

"Better let me do that. Here, you hold Dory."

"I'm capable of mixing formula."

"I didn't say you weren't."

"You implied it. Look, Dave, just because you've had a child and I haven't doesn't mean—"

"Let's not argue about baby bottles. You fix the bottle, I'll take her to my shop and—"

"Oh, no, she's my responsibility. I'll feed her right here."

"I have more time than you at the moment. Peter's at the store today—"

"I can manage. Help's on the way. Mrs. Wilcox can give me a couple days a week." She reached for Dory, but Dave pulled back.

"You have fudgeballs to make and all those blue ribbons to tie."

Jenny sank onto the nearest bench. "Please don't say blue. It's *Floridian.*"

They both laughed, and the tension subsided. It was hard to refuse him when he looked at her with those puppy-dog eyes. He seemed so happy with Dory, and she needed her hands free.

"Okay, *you* feed the baby, and I'll wrap fudge-balls."

Dave grinned. "Deal." He glanced at Dory. "I haven't had breakfast with a woman this pretty in a long time."

THAT EVENING, Jenny sat down to rock Dory. The day had been hectic beyond belief. She knew she should be working on the financial statement, but the baby felt so good in her arms. She hugged Dory's warm, cuddly body close. Now she knew why people had babies. So they could rock them. The gentle back and forth, back and forth dissolved the cares of the day. Dory had drifted off to sleep, but Jenny couldn't lay her down yet. If she did, she would have to quit rocking—and rocking was nice.

She hummed a lullaby her mother used to sing to her. "Mama's gonna buy you a something, something." She had forgotten the words but not the tune. She smiled at Dory, who was making sucking motions with her sweet mouth. "And if that something doesn't something, Mama's gonna buy you a something else."

Mama. The word felt natural on her tongue.

Would she ever be a mama? She squeezed Dory tighter. If Rob and Teensy didn't come back, she would—by default. If that were to happen, would she be able to keep the child? Dave was right. Authorities would eventually have to be notified. The thought made her queasy. She refused to believe Rob would be so coldhearted.

It would be hard to assume responsibility for the infant without risking the expansion of Fudgeballs. Motherhood wasn't factored into the next few months of her life. She hated to admit it, but Dave had been so helpful lately she almost hated to see him leave.

He was right about her knowing nothing about babies. A mortgage and picket fence were high on her list of priorities. But finding the right man to share her dream wasn't that simple, and her life was too hectic to go looking.

She pushed against the floor with her slippered feet and nudged the rocker in motion again. Sometimes life was downright complicated.

DAVE CLOSED the cash register, then sacked the customer's purchases. On the other side of the wall, he could hear Dory screaming at the top of her lungs. Teething, he decided. Lower incisors. Always an ugly experience. Then upper incisors. Really nasty.

Jake sent up a loud howl as Dory screeched. Darn that dog. He'd started sympathizing with the baby's wails, making the situation worse. Tourists steered clear of the racket.

Dave stepped to the door. "Knock it off, Jake!"

Jake looked up, lifted his head and howled louder.

"Thanks." The customer pocketed his change. "That dog out there sure can howl." The fiftyish man looked in the sack before closing it.

"I'm afraid my dog's decided he's in love with the baby next door." Grabbing an empty foam cup, Dave followed the patron out the front door. The man continued down the street as Dave made a ninety-degree turn into Fudgeballs. Jenny glanced up as he entered.

He lifted the foam cup. "Ran out of coffee. Have an extra cup?"

"Just made a fresh pot." She motioned toward the back room. "Help yourself. Are you aware your dog is howling like a banshee?"

"He's sympathizing with Dory." He walked over

to tickle Dory on the belly. "What's all the crying? Is she teething?"

"I haven't the slightest idea. She's been like this all morning."

Dave frowned when he saw the dark circles shadowing Jenny's eyes.

"Rough night?"

"No, Dory slept like a—"

"Baby?" Dave guessed.

Jenny nodded. "It was shortly after breakfast when she turned militant."

Dave poked a finger in the corner of the infant's diaper. "She's dry."

"Dry, fed, pampered, rocked—I'm at the end of my list."

Grinning, Dave picked up Dory and put her on his shoulder. This he could handle. When Megan was little, he took care of her more than Nancy did. Nancy was more concerned with her bridge club and country club than motherhood—all in the pursuit of networking, she'd insisted. At least her lack of interest in their daughter had taught him the finer arts of fatherhood. Arts he dearly missed. He hadn't given the smell of baby powder and formula burps much thought until Dory brought memories of Megan. Talking baby gibberish, he waltzed Dory around the room until her frantic screams dissolved into soft, hiccuping snubs.

Wiping her hands on her apron, Jenny came around the counter to stare at him. "How'd you do that?"

"Practice. Megan cried the entire first year of her life. Dory's definitely teething. Heard anything from

Rob?'' Dave gently patted Dory's back as her eyelids started to droop.

''Not a thing.'' Jenny returned to stirring the boiling kettle.

''Where's your hired help?''

''Mrs. Wilcox is due in any moment.'' She dumped sugar and corn syrup into a second kettle. ''The baby's been cranky, and I'm so behind it's scary. Sorry I can't take time to visit.''

Dory was fast asleep, and he tenderly lowered her into the carrier. Outside, Jake's howls faded to simpering whines.

''Thank goodness,'' Jenny said in response to the blissful silence.

''You don't like my dog, do you?''

''About as much as you like mine.'' She grinned.

Moving quietly away from the carrier, Dave motioned toward the back room. ''Should I take her back there?''

''Would you?'' She was afraid she looked so grateful he felt sorry for her. ''Put her where I can see her—and be sure and wrap her blanket tightly around her little feet so they won't get cold.''

''It's summer. She'll get too hot.''

''I don't want her coming down with the sniffles.''

Dave returned a moment later with a cup of coffee. Leaning against the counter, he took a sip as he watched her work. She looked cute in the oversize T-shirt with the sleeves rolled up. It hung loose to the bottom of her Bermuda shorts, covering the small waistline he'd admired more than once. Strands of hair fell from the ponytail to caress her neck, some-

thing he'd like to do himself. "What do you intend
to say when people notice Rob and Teensy are gone,
and Dory's with you?"

"The truth. Rob left Dory with me while he and
Teensy took a few days off."

Dave shook his head. "You really think they're
coming back?"

"I don't know—I haven't the time to worry about
it right now."

He followed her to the front case where she slid in
a pan of maple walnut. "Think you can get away for
a few minutes after work?"

"I don't know—why?"

"I talked to a Realtor this morning. He says there's
a building in Mackinac City for rent. Perfect location,
good retail space. How about it? Want to look at it
with me?"

She picked up a bolt of blue ribbon and moved to
the worktable. "You think it sounds promising?"

"It sounds promising."

"And you want us to look at it? Together?"

He shrugged. "Recalling our earlier conversation
about wanting to expand..."

He was trying to make this easy for her. His conscience wouldn't let him take her space without
knowing she had a place to go. He'd contacted a
Realtor in Mackinac City, and now he hoped nature
would take its course.

"Oh." She started wrapping fudgeballs. "You
want me to look at it with you."

"I can get away—can you?" He noticed a blush
colored her cheeks, and she refused to look at him.

How much easier did she want it? He usually didn't go to such lengths to accommodate a former tenant, but she was different. His gaze slid over her breasts. Unfortunately, dammit, a lot different.

She finally glanced at him with a coy smile. He didn't know her well, but she was acting strange. Was he imagining the spark between them? No, he definitely felt something—something that spelled trouble. The casual businesslike rapport he'd tried hard to maintain seemed to be slipping.

"I can get away shortly after five-thirty—if that's not too late?"

"No," he said, then repeated, "no. Five-thirty would be great. I'll call the Realtor and let him know we'll be there a little after six."

"We'll have to take Dory."

"No problem. If you're game, we'll get a bite to eat when we're through." Getting her settled would take a load off his mind, and it would be nice to have a dinner companion.

"I'm game." She straightened, working a kink out of her lower back. "It's awfully nice of you to move so quickly on this."

"Don't mention it. I know you want to expand as soon as possible." She looked relieved, and he was glad he'd taken the initiative.

"I do—and I really appreciate you taking time to help out, especially since you're busy, too."

Dave waved her gratitude aside, eyeing the wisps of blue ribbon littering the work table. "Is that the Floridian blue you promised?"

She glanced at the bolts of ribbon and mounds of yet-to-be-wrapped fudgeballs, sighing. "Yes."

"It's none of my business, but isn't that closer to Indiana purple?" he joked.

She took a closer look at the ribbon. Cripes. Of course it was wrong. Why hadn't she noticed the purplish cast? "It's Federal blue," she said, appalled at the mistake.

"Really?" He picked up a fudgeball and examined the cellophane wrap. "I was thinking more like *Nightmare on Elm Street.*"

Her face fell. "It is bright, isn't it?"

"What's it going to be used for?"

"A debutante's coming-out party."

He took a sip of coffee. "If you want to get another color, I'll watch the store until your help gets here." He smiled. "There's going to be one unhappy debutante if you stay with that color."

"Mrs. Sagan-Meyer would kill me if it was anything other than what she ordered." She hurriedly stripped off her apron. "What about the kite shop?"

"I'll hang a sign saying I'll be back in half an hour."

Giving her appearance a once-over in the mirror, she smoothed her hair, then reached for her purse. "I won't be long."

"Take your time."

He watched her leave and sipped his coffee. He was pleased with himself. If all went well, his troubles were over. He could expand the kite shop with a clear conscience, knowing Fudgeballs would continue to thrive in the new location. He wasn't an ogre, just a businessman. It was satisfying to know he and Jenny would part as friends.

He smiled at his brilliance. He knew how to handle women, with the notable exception of Nancy. He sobered. A Sumo wrestler would have a tough time pinning her to the mat.

The expansion was proceeding like a well-oiled piece of machinery. By tonight, McNeill would have her new floor space, and he could get on with his plans.

If he could only find Megan, things would be perfect.

4

FIVE-THIRTY that afternoon, Jenny carried Dory aboard Shepler's ferry for the sixteen-minute hydroplane ride to Mackinac City. Dave struggled behind, loaded down with a diaper bag, stroller and a folded baby blanket big enough to cover half of Mackinac Island. Jenny was afraid the baby would be cold on the ride back.

They stood at the railing, laughing with Dory as she delighted in the outing.

The wind whipped their hair as the boat skimmed across the top of the water. Jenny smiled. It was the first time she'd ever seen one strand of his dark blond hair out of place. She tried to hold down the bottom of her sundress. It would be embarrassing to have it blow in her face. She hated dresses, but she was glad she'd kept one in the back room for emergencies. For once she felt like a lady next to him. He'd always seen her in shorts and T-shirts, and she wondered if he'd even noticed her dress. In the distance, Mackinac Bridge, one of the largest suspension bridges in the United States, glistened in the sun.

Dory reached over and latched onto Dave's hair, yanking it. He rewarded her with a playful yelp, and she yanked harder, showing two reddened spots on her lower gums where the beginnings of a tiny new tooth had suddenly appeared.

"Oh, Dave, look!" Dory bucked and squirmed, averting her head as Jenny tried to probe the new addition. "Her first tooth!"

Dave steadied the baby's head over squealing protests as they examined the tooth with parental pride.

"It's going to be so straight!" Jenny exclaimed.

"Have you ever seen an eight-month-old in braces?"

"No, silly—but it looks exceptionally good, don't you think?"

"It's perfect." He pretended to throw Dory up in the air and catch her. The baby burst into giggles.

"Rob and Teensy are going to be heartsick they missed this moment." Jenny leaned against the railing, luxuriating in the feel of the wind through her hair. She'd worn it loose for a change, knowing it would never stay in a ponytail during the boat ride. She'd caught Dave staring at her when he thought she wasn't looking.

"You have a camera?"

"At home. Why?"

"A first tooth is—what do they say on television? A Kodak moment?"

Why, the old softy, Jenny thought. *He's sentimental.* Cocking her head, she smiled. "As in, We'll take a picture so Rob and Teensy can share in the fun when they get back?"

"As in, It's cute. Let's remember it."

He didn't believe Rob and Teensy would be back. She refused to believe they wouldn't. Her only problem was to keep her role of temporary guardian in perspective, or she would find herself head over heels in love with Dory and be crushed when she had to give her up.

The ferry docked, and they walked the short distance to where a late-model Mustang convertible, hunter green with tan top, was parked.

"Nice car," she commented.

"Thanks." He strapped Dory's carrier into the back seat.

Jenny glanced around the car. "I used to keep my Volkswagen Beetle parked here, but I sold it a couple of years ago. I just didn't use it that much."

It was close to six when they entered Alstairs Realty. Cool air seeped through Jenny's thin cotton dress. A tall, distinguished-looking gray-haired man with a mustache got up from his desk to shake hands with Dave.

"Right on time."

Dave smiled. "How's it going, Loyal?"

"Can't complain." His friendly gaze shifted. "And this must be Jenny McNeill."

Jenny smiled, switching Dory to her opposite hip to shake hands.

The Realtor was all smiles. "McNeill? Were you related to Millie McNeill?"

"Millie was my grandmother. After her death, I stayed on at the cottage where I grew up and decided to open Fudgeballs."

He chuckled. "What a small world. Millie used to play bridge with my sister, Leona."

"Leona was your sister? She was Gram's best friend. How is she?"

"Leona's in a nursing home now, but doing pretty good." His brows lifted.

"Millie could sure tell stories."

Jenny smiled, remembering. "She sure could."

"Dave says your fudgeballs rival Godiva chocolates."

Jenny blushed. "Thanks, but it's hard to beat a Godiva."

Preliminaries aside, Loyal tickled Dory under her chin. "You've sure got a cute baby. What's this little charmer's name?"

"Dory's not mine. I'm watching her for a friend."

Loyal took the disclaimer in stride. "Well, I know you're anxious to look at the property. Relocating, huh?"

Jenny glanced at Dave, smiling. "Dave says it's a nice location."

"A real honey." Loyal took a set of keys off a peg. "It's only a block away."

Dave took Dory as they left the air-conditioned office and stepped into the eighty-five-degree evening. Heat shimmered from the sidewalk and crept up her bare legs.

Dave unfolded the stroller and settled Dory in for the short walk. The baby fussed. Jenny had given her a bottle just before they left the shop, but it was getting close to her dinnertime.

Dave tried to cajole away the infant's sudden foul mood by pointing out her reflection in the windowpanes as they passed. Dory was only momentarily distracted.

Loyal unlocked the door of an attractive-looking storefront. As they stepped into the building's interior, Jenny visualized colorful kites hanging from the ceiling and tacked on the walls. There was plenty of space for counters and display racks. Her excitement rose. The place was perfect for Dave.

"There's twenty-five hundred square feet, ample lighting—everything a business needs," Loyal said. "Foot traffic is good, maybe not quite as good as on the island during peak times, but good."

Dave meandered to the back of the store where a bathroom and two small rooms were located. "There's plenty of room for an office and storage."

Jenny joined him to peek in the largest room. "I like the layout—good view of the front door."

"A person could get—what, Loyal? Five or six display cases in a room this size?"

"At least that—maybe more."

Dave grinned at Jenny. "Room for a lot of fudge."

"Or kites," she agreed, laughing. As far as she was concerned, it was the ideal location for him. Even if there wasn't as much foot traffic as the island offered, with the new line of Space Alien kites and word of mouth, Dave would have all the business he could handle.

They wandered around the store, pointing out advantages and disadvantages, but in general agreed the building was ideal for expansion.

"So," Dave asked, taking Dory out of the stroller. He smiled at the baby. "What do you think?"

Dory gurgled, latching onto Dave's hair again.

"Well, I like it," Jenny said. "What do you think?"

"I think it's ideal."

"Good." Loyal opened his briefcase. "Shall I draw up the contract?"

Dave glanced at Jenny.

She glanced at him.

When she saw he seemed to be hesitating, she said, "I don't think you could go wrong, do you?"

"No. It's got all the space a person could want."

She smiled. "Indeed." She waited for him to clinch the deal. If he signed the contract now, he could be out of his side of the unit by the end of the month. The timing couldn't be better.

When she glanced up, she saw Dave and Loyal staring at her. Her hand went to her hair, suddenly aware of her appearance. Was there something wrong with her dress? She hadn't worn panty hose, only comfortable sandals. She should have slipped into the bathroom and at least run a comb through her hair. The ferry ride had been windy. Why were they staring?

When no one said anything, the silence grew unbearable.

"Price is right," she offered, hoping to get on with it. She was hungry.

Dave nodded. "Can't beat it for the floor space."

Silence.

Clearing his throat, Dave glanced at Loyal. "Why don't I give you a call in the morning."

"Certainly." Loyal closed the briefcase. "I'll be in and out all day. Just leave a message if I'm gone."

They parted outside the building, Loyal going one way, Dave and Jenny the other. Jenny wondered why Dave hadn't jumped on the opportunity. It wasn't the money. That part didn't seem to worry him. Maybe he didn't want to discuss finances in front of her. Retail space like this didn't come along every day. Good location, easy access—she'd given her seal of approval. She couldn't appear overanxious, but he needed to move, and quickly, or he'd lose the location.

"You like Italian food?" Dave's voice jerked her back.

"Sure. Anything. I'm not particular."

Jenny was amazed by how happy Dave seemed. He sang a song to Dory and laughed as he pushed the stroller to the restaurant on the corner. He held the door for her, then entered with Dory, parking the stroller beside the coatrack.

"I'll take her," Jenny said as the waitress approached with menus.

Dave handed Dory over with a smile and followed Jenny to the table, his hand resting on her shoulder as they walked. The waitress brought a high chair and they ordered.

"So what do you think?" It was a simple yes-or-no question, but he proceeded to talk nonstop about the positive aspects of the building and how nice it would be to have all that space.

Finally the food arrived and silence prevailed as they ate. Dory enjoyed the bites of spaghetti Jenny smashed into a pulp. Banging a spoon on the high chair, the baby drew an occasional reprimanding look from nearby diners.

Jenny wrestled the spoon away from her, then took her to the ladies' room to clean and change her. When she returned, Dory's head was nodding.

Laying Dory in the booth beside her, Jenny smiled as the baby stared at her with eyes so like Rob's. Her heart turned over. So much for not getting attached, she thought. Dory blinked a couple of times, then dropped off to sleep.

Resting her head on the back of the booth, Jenny closed her eyes. She felt the chill of a wineglass being placed in her right hand and smiled.

"You're going to make a damn good mother."

"I love children," she murmured, taking a sip of the wine he'd thoughtfully poured. Dave Kasada knew how to please a woman. Rehashing the subject of the new space crossed her mind, but she decided for once to forget business. She was in the company of a good-looking man, the baby was asleep, the hectic day was finally over. It felt good to drift for awhile.

"Rough day?"

"The worst—but they've all been that way lately."

"Mrs. Wilcox working out?"

"She eats more than she sells."

They shared a smile. How long had it been since she'd been alone with a man? She couldn't remember. She'd dated a few times since the breakup with Brian, but eligible men on the island were at a premium. There was Jay Matson, the golf pro. Terry Black, dull but nice. Rick Collier, a man who loved *all* women.

Dave toyed with his glass, obviously at ease with the moment. How many hearts had *he* broken? A few, she'd guess. Had he instigated his divorce, or had it been his wife? Why? Incompatible, fell out of love, outgrew each other? She thanked God for Brian's cold feet. They might have married, and she could be in Dave's position, divorced, hurt, fighting for a child.

"Ever been married, Jenny?"

She glanced up, surprised he was attuned to her thoughts. "No. Came close once."

"What happened?"

"He couldn't commit. I think he wanted to, but something inside wouldn't let him."

"That's pretty unbiased for a woman."

She shrugged, gazing at the bottom of her glass. Candlelight turned the ruby red liquid into a shimmering pool. "I don't think Brian would agree with you. I was pretty hard on him—resented the seven years I lost with him. It hurt then, but I'm getting over it now."

"Does anyone ever get over something like that?" He took a sip of wine.

Sensing his disappointment, she reached out and laid her hand on his. The contact was warm and assuring. "One mistake doesn't give me—or you—the right to say all relationships are bad."

He stared at the table. "Philosophy?"

"Bunk." She grinned and bit into a breadstick. "But it sounds good, doesn't it?"

He stared into his glass. "I'm glad you can make light of it. It hasn't been that easy for me. When

Nancy and I split up, I didn't think I'd have to fight tooth and nail to see my daughter, but that's the way it's turned out.''

"I'm sorry. Divorce stinks. When children are involved, it's even harder.''

His gaze met hers across the table. "I love Megan. I don't want her to grow up and never know me. Is that so wrong? I didn't divorce Megan, I divorced Nancy. There's a hell of a lot of difference. I lay awake nights worrying about my daughter.'' He dug in his back pocket and brought out his billfold. "Want to see a picture of my little girl?''

She took it from him.

A small blond-haired child sat beside a striking brunette. The diamond on Nancy's well-manicured finger must have cost a small fortune.

"She's beautiful—both of them, for that matter.'' Jenny ran her fingers through her hair as she looked at the photograph. "I must look a mess.''

"You look good.'' His gaze softened. "I like your hair down like that.''

He laid his hand over hers. Brian's touch seemed like a boy's next to Dave's. It wasn't fair to compare Dave to Brian—there was no comparison. Not in looks, attitude or the way she reacted to him. The concern in his eyes made her want to strangle his ex-wife. It seemed grossly unfair to use the child as a pawn. Obviously, Nancy knew where to strike and what would hurt him most.

"Don't worry. It takes time to locate a missing person. Perhaps if you relax and give it another week or two.'' If anything bad happened, you'd be notified.'' She covered the rim of her glass, shaking her head when the waiter was about to refill it.

Pushing his glass aside, Dave pulled a credit card out of his billfold and laid it on the check tray. The waiter disappeared.

"Sorry to be such bad company," he apologized. "I guess being with Dory this week has brought back memories of when Megan was a baby."

"I understand." Jenny gazed at the sleeping infant. "At least you have a daughter." She was thirty-one and not even close to motherhood.

THE WINE made Jenny sleepy. On the ferry ride home, she leaned on his shoulder and dozed. Dave glanced at Dory and adjusted her head more comfortably on his lap.

He sobered, thinking about Megan. How many times had she lain on his lap, sleeping? Tendrils of blond hair framing wide, innocent blue eyes. God, he missed her so much it hurt. Was she all right? Was Nancy off on another one of her jaunts with her newest lover? He wouldn't put it past her. Consideration wasn't her strong suit.

His gaze moved to Jenny, snoring softly. He grinned. She'd freak if she knew what she was doing. Especially in front of him. The grin faded. He liked her. Not only liked her, he was feeling an attraction he hadn't felt for a woman in a long time.

Why hadn't she rented the building tonight? She'd liked it. She wasn't just saying so to make him happy. She had no idea he wanted her space. Word of mouth would keep her business thriving. She might even think about franchising her product. There wasn't another fudge shop around that could match her.

Was money tight? He should have asked. He gently lifted a lock of hair off her face. Hell, he could foot the first year's rent and let her pay it back at her convenience. Should he offer? No. She was a nineties woman. She'd make it on her own or she wouldn't make it at all. His mind drifted to Brian, the man she had wanted to marry. Why would a man have a hard time committing to her?

The ferry docked, and Jenny roused. She sat up, looked around, blinked sleepily, then blushed. "Did I fall asleep?"

"For a few minutes."

"Did I...snore?"

He laughed and didn't want to embarrass her. "You were so quiet, I shook you once to see if you were still alive."

She breathed a sigh of relief. "I shouldn't have had so much wine. It always wipes me out."

"Tell you what." Dave handed her the blanket, then picked up Dory in one arm, the stroller and diaper bag in the other. "Why don't I take Dory home with me tonight? There's a baby crib in the upstairs guest room. Aunt Mosie insisted she have one when Megan was little."

"Oh, Dave..."

He saw her reluctance and tried to ease her concerns. "You could get a good night's sleep. And it would be nice to have a baby in the house again."

"That wouldn't seem right. Rob left Dory with me."

"I'm a responsible adult. Let me help you, Jenny. You're tired, and it's late. I'll enjoy the company."

She looked unconvinced.

"Are you sure? She's up at least a couple of times a night...." She trailed behind him as they left the boat, listing all the things that could go wrong.

"I can handle whatever comes up." When she covered her mouth in a series of yawns, he could see she was softening. He sweetened the pot. "You can sleep late in the morning."

That sealed it. He doubted she'd had over four hours' sleep since Rob had left Dory on her doorstep.

When they parted at the end of the peer, she kissed Dory goodbye. "See you in the morning, sweetie."

"I'll be here," Dave teased.

"Not you." She punched his arm, yawning again. "If the slightest thing goes wrong, you call me. Understand?"

"It's pretty complicated, but I think I've got it."

"And she likes oatmeal for breakfast."

"Got it."

She released a sigh. "Thanks, Dave. I'm going to bed."

"See you in the morning."

She walked off, then suddenly turned and called, "She likes to be rocked!"

Dave nodded. "Who doesn't?"

He watched her disappear into the shadows, admiring the curve of her hips. She wasn't overly thin, like some women. He liked that.

Better idea—we can send Dory home and you can stay all night with me.

"Hey, Jenny?"

"Yes?" Her voice came back to him.

"What about the building we looked at? You like it?"

"I love it!"

He grinned. "I'll call Loyal in the morning."

"Great!"

"WE'VE ALL GOT PROBLEMS, Sam!" Dave stuffed scrambled eggs into Dory's mouth. She spat it at him. He should have made oatmeal, but he didn't have any. "How can they always be two steps ahead of you?" Angry heat spread up his face. "I've already missed Megan's birthday, and at the rate you're going, I'll miss Christmas! No more excuses. Give me something positive!" He slammed the receiver down.

Wiping a hand over his face, he took a deep breath. He hadn't been this frustrated since his last court battle with Nancy.

Dory stared at him solemnly.

"Want some bananas?"

She giggled, kicking her feet.

As he spooned strained fruit in her mouth, he rifled through kite orders. Why couldn't he be as successful with women as he was with business? Then life would be good.

He had an odd feeling about Nancy and her sudden disappearance. It was unusual even for her. She wasn't one to think of his feelings, but neither had she ever completely gone back on her word about leaving Megan with him.

He reached for the receiver and dialed Alstairs

Realtors. A woman's voice answered, and he asked for Loyal.

"Loyal? Dave Kasada."

"Dave! I was hoping to hear from you."

"Well, she loves the space. Why don't you get a contract ready. She'll most likely be contacting you later today."

"Sure thing. How long a lease will she want?"

"You'll have to talk to her—I just want to make sure the space doesn't get away."

"I'll take care of it."

"Thanks, Loyal."

He hung up then carried Dory into the bathroom. Stripping off her soiled nightie, he winked. "Most women look sallow in bananas. Fruit looks good on you."

JENNY GLANCED UP from the copper kettle as Dave walked into the shop around nine. "Hi, I was getting worried about you. How's Dory this morning?"

He looked like Kevin Costner first thing in the morning. She looked like Courtney Love before she became a movie star. Jenny had worked on the financial report until three. This morning she'd overslept. She'd barely had time to jump into the shower and dab on a little lipstick. She peeled off the plastic gloves and self-consciously smoothed her hair into place. It was still damp. With the natural curl, she probably looked like Princess.

Dave set the baby carrier down. "She's a little out of sorts—that tooth's bothering her."

Jenny wiped her hands on her apron and took the baby from him. "Did you get any sleep at all?"

"Some. I bought a teething ring and iced it down in the freezer. It seemed to help. Tonight I'll—"

"You can't keep her tonight."

"Why not?"

"Because you just can't. Rob left her with me." She realized how juvenile that sounded, but she wanted Dory with her. Hang the financial reports and Fudgeballs. "I'm getting caught up with my orders." She nuzzled Dory. "I've missed you, sweetie." Dory grabbed Jenny's finger, stuck it in her mouth and clamped down hard. Jenny sucked in her breath and grinned when she felt something sharp. "Dave!" She probed the front gums, grinning. "She's got *two* teeth!"

Dave was instantly at her side, poking his finger in Dory's mouth. "I'll be damned, there *are* two. Where did the second one come from? It wasn't there last night."

Jenny felt giddy. It was a momentous occasion. "Here, hold her while I get the camera."

She was aware of his gaze following her to the back room. She didn't have to look at him to sense his interest. The tingling sensation down her spine told her he was looking at her as a woman rather than a neighbor. She had to keep her distance. The more she was around him, the more she enjoyed his company. Her growing interest and dependence scared her.

She returned a moment later. "I found it, and it still has film. We're in luck."

Dave exchanged the baby for the camera. "I'll get a shot of you holding Dory."

"Not the way I look," she protested.

"You're gorgeous. Hold Dory's mouth open."

It took several tries to get the pose just right. Jenny tickled Dory's belly to make her laugh just before Dave snapped the picture. She was still giggling with Dory when she handed the baby to him. "Now you."

Their hands brushed as they made the switch. She was certain Dave's fingers lingered longer than necessary. Or was it that when they touched, everything moved in slow motion? Heat spread to parts of her body she'd purposely ignored since her breakup with Brian. Was it her imagination, or did she sense reluctance when his hand left hers? She didn't need this complication in her life. He obviously wasn't in the market for a relationship, and she had enough to contend with without falling in love.

"All right, now let me get a shot of you," she teased.

"Me?" Dave frowned. "Forget it. I hate having my picture taken."

"Too bad!" She grinned, lifting the camera.

He lowered Dory in front of him till the top of her head was at his chin, crossed his eyes and stuck his tongue out the side of his mouth just as the flash went off.

"That'll be one she can show to her grandkids," Jenny grumbled.

Dory began sucking her fist and whimpering.

"Is she hungry?" She laid the camera on the counter.

"No, I just fed her." Dave lifted the baby over his shoulder and patted her. "I'll take her to the house and put her down for a nap. Peter's watching the store this morning."

Jenny stiffened. He was doing it again. All of a sudden he was taking care of Dory and she wasn't. "No. I know you're more experienced, but I think I'm doing just fine for a beginner."

"You're doing a great job, but you're busy and I'm not."

Jenny rounded the display case. "I don't mean to sound ungrateful. You've been a big help, but I can take it from here. I've imposed enough as it is. I really shouldn't have involved you."

The door opened, and a stream of customers poured in. They spread out, crowding the small floor space.

Jenny tried to take Dory from him.

He held on tightly.

She pulled at Dory, and Dory fussed louder.

Dave drew back. "You're hurting her."

"Then let go of her."

"She needs a nap, for heaven's sake. What's the big deal about me taking her to my house and putting her down for a nap?"

"She isn't yours!"

"She isn't yours, either."

"Stop this, Dave." Her eyes narrowed. "*I* will take care of her."

"You've got a store full of customers and no help. Don't be stubborn about this."

"Don't you be stubborn! Mrs. Wilcox will be here

any moment." They locked horns, their gazes fixed and determined.

"Excuse me?" A woman with three children stood by the register waiting to pay for her purchases. "Is anyone working here?"

Jenny caught her breath. Her eyes fixed on Dave's fingers, making tiny circles on the baby's back. She imagined his hand on her back. She blinked the disturbing image away.

Stop it, her head screamed. *Stop looking at him that way and thinking of him that way.* She was so close to achieving financial security, so close to fulfilling her dreams for Fudgeballs. She couldn't throw a monkey wrench in the works by getting emotionally involved with him. She couldn't.

"Dave, go home. You're not needed anymore. I can handle it from here." Blunt and to the point was the only sensible way to handle the matter.

Disbelief, then hurt flickered in his eyes.

"Jenny—"

Taking Dory from him, she ignored the disappointment in his tone. Tough love. She'd heard of it, just never put it to use. She stepped around him and carried Dory into the back room.

When she returned a moment later, he was gone.

Swallowing the knot in her throat, she pasted a smile on her face and waited on customers.

5

PRINCESS DIPPED HER HEAD to stare at the sleeping bulldog. *"Mon ami?"*

Jake opened one eye, yawned and licked his chops. "Huh? What'd ya call me?"

"Mon ami. I called you my friend."

"Friend? Since when?" Jake shifted to his other side to resume his nap.

Princess nudged his backside with her nose. "Come play with me."

Jake raised his head. "Play? With you?" He sat up and looked at her. "Are you nuts? You're askin' *me* to play with *you?* One minute I'm barred from looking at you, the next you want to play?"

Tears welled in her eyes, and she swiped them away with her paw.

"Aw, shoot. What are you bawlin' for? What'd I do?"

"I am lonely, monsieur."

He rose, shook and strutted around her, giving her a couple of sniffs. "You been drinkin' something stronger than water?"

She laid down, put her head between her paws and whined.

"Okay, okay—quit your bellyachin'. I'll play.

What'll it be? Chase?'' He jumped at her, pulled back and jumped again.

She didn't move. He put a paw on her back and gave her a shove. "You wanted to play, let's play."

"I don't feel like it anymore."

Jake snorted, hiked his leg on the tree, then settled in his former spot. Poodles!

Princess let out a mournful whimper. "Talk to me."

Good grief. "What do you want me to say?"

She turned away. "If you don't know, then I'm not going to tell you. *Don't* talk to me."

Jake pushed himself to a sitting position. "Is this a game? Play with me—don't play with me. Talk to me—don't talk to me. You missing a few kibbles?"

Princess let out a wail.

Jake shot up like a bullet. "Oh, for cryin' out loud. *Now* what'd I say?"

"I haven't gotten one kibble treat since the baby came," Princess sniffed.

Jake snorted and licked his nose. "Is that all? That's nothin' to cry about. That chunk o' nothin' wouldn't fill a hollow tooth." *I could give her back her bone. Nah.*

He rummaged in his dog dish for a scrap of leftovers and came up with a piece of crust off Dave's bologna sandwich. "Here." He laid the morsel on the ground in front of her. "Now *this* is something you can sink your teeth into."

Princess sprang to her feet and strutted to her cushion. "I'm not hungry!"

Jake followed her. "Am I missing something here?"

"You couldn't understand—you have a human who loves you."

"Dave? Sure, he's a good guy." He laid down beside her cushion. "Your human loves you."

"Alas, she has forgotten me." She sighed.

"Forgotten you? How could anyone forget you, yippin' and yappin' all the time, leapin' around like a Mexican jumping bean—"

Her wails stopped him. "She only has time for the baby now."

Jake rolled onto his back and wiggled to give it a good scratch. "Now I get the picture. You're jealous."

Princess sat up. "I am *not!*" She stuck her nose in the air. "Well, perhaps a bit, but I love the baby, too."

"Well, I like the kid, but the humans are gaga over it. I, for one, haven't had a decent nap since she got here." He snorted. "All that fussin' and squallin'."

"True, monsieur. Jenny can't get anything done for changing diapers, mixing formula and rocking—constantly rocking. And *your* human is always underfoot, wanting to play with Dory. I never get lap time anymore."

"Oh, you know humans," Jake said, "they'll get around to us eventually." He sprang to his feet and panted. "Dry your eyes, tootsie. I can get your mind off your troubles—let's wrestle!"

JENNY BLEW a wayward strand of hair from her forehead as she coaxed Dory to take a bite of strained spinach. "I know it looks bad, sweetie, but it's good for you. Just one little bite."

Dory grabbed the spoon and flung it across the room, spattering green globs over Jenny's clean T-shirt, the floor, the counter and a new batch of black walnut fudge.

"Oh, Dory, not again." Frustrated, she called for Mrs. Wilcox. "I need help up here!"

The chubby woman shuffled in from the back room, carrying a sack of sugar in one hand and stuffing fudgeballs into her mouth with the other. She swallowed hard then licked her fingers.

"Thought I'd start another batch of chocolate. We're running a little low."

"Already?" Jenny glanced at the sparse selection in the candy case. Three days on the job, and already Mrs. Wilcox had eaten her way through two trays of chocolate. "Well, go ahead. I'll get this mess cleaned up, then try to get Dory down for her nap while you're mixing another batch."

"Yum." Mrs. Wilcox pinched off a piece of the spattered fudge. "Don't throw this out. I'll take it home. The mister won't mind a little spinach."

Surrounded by Dory's fussy crying, Mrs. Wilcox spread the recipe in front of her and began pouring ingredients into the copper kettle. Jenny bounced the baby on one hip while wiping strained baby food from the counter and watching the older woman pluck up a handful of the remaining fudgeballs from the case and pop them into her mouth.

"Sure is a colicky baby," Mrs. Wilcox said, her cheek bulging with candy.

"I don't know what's wrong with her. Nothing suits her. She won't eat, won't sleep. I've tried everything," Jenny replied, admittedly at her wits end.

"Try a little clove oil on her gums."

Jenny hoisted Dory to her shoulder and patted her back, trying to hear Mrs. Wilcox above Dory's wails. "Clove what on where?"

"Teething's hard on the little mites," the woman said, giving the chocolate concoction a hefty stir. "Need to put a little clove oil on your finger and rub it on her gums. Should feel good to her."

Before Jenny had a chance to thank her for the advice, Mrs. Wilcox ate the last fudgeball on the tray then smiled. "I've a bit of a sweet tooth."

Jenny lamely returned the smile. "I'm going to ask Dave to watch her while I run to the pharmacy for the clove oil. Can you handle things here?"

Dave had avoided her the past couple of days. Who could blame him? She'd been rude and insensitive when she'd told him he wasn't needed. She missed his advice—and his help. As much as she hated the thought, she had to apologize.

"Oh, no problem. Candy makin' is right up my alley. I've made tons of it in my lifetime."

Jenny nodded. "Well, as soon as you get that batch done, start another. I have a large order to fill."

Dory whimpered. "Hush, sweetie." Jenny stuck the pacifier in the baby's mouth, and Dory immediately spat it out and cried harder. Lifting her to her shoulder, she patted the baby's back while turning to Mrs. Wilcox. "I won't be gone long."

Mrs. Wilcox sampled her concoction by pouring a ladleful onto a saucer and eating it with a spoon. "Just right," she announced to Jenny, who was gaping at the amount of sweets the woman could consume.

"EXCUSE ME? I'm not needed, remember?" Dave gave Jenny a sour look as he took the wriggling Dory from her. "Hi, Munchkin. Still having trouble with those ol' toofies?"

Dory gave him a wide, drooly grin.

"Her toofies are killing us both. I know I said I didn't need you, but I apologize. I do need your help, and I'm sorry I was so rude. Mrs. Wilcox says clove oil will help Dory's teething, and I don't have any."

Who does, other than a leftover pioneer?

"I can't leave the baby with Mrs. Wilcox. It's all she can do to wait on customers. Can you watch her while I run up to the pharmacy and buy the oil?"

Dave bounced the infant on his shoulder. "Sure, I'll watch her. Take your time."

"Thanks." She turned toward the door, relieved he was being so generous.

"Heard from Rob and Teensy?"

"No, but I'm sure I will any day now."

Actually, she wasn't so sure anymore. A week had gone by without a word from the parents. Was it possible Rob didn't intend to come back? She shoved the flicker of hope aside. Dory needed her parents. But Jenny couldn't deny she would welcome the chance to keep Dory. Forever. With each passing day, the child grew more important to her. She was the first thing she saw in the morning, and the last thing she saw at night. The baby lay beside her in bed, giggling as Jenny counted toes and tiny little fingers, the smell of baby powder sweet in the air. She sympathized with Dave. How could he bear to be apart from the little daughter he'd helped create? She'd like to ask him about Megan, but the shop was full of customers.

He stepped closer and bent toward her. "You don't sound as positive as you did a week ago."

"Maybe because I'm not."

He motioned toward the back room. "Want to talk about it?"

She shook her head. "I'm not making any decisions yet. There's plenty of time for panic."

"Come on, Jenny, be sensible. You can't keep the child. Children can't be given away. They have laws about those things. The authorities will have to be notified."

Jenny glanced at Dory, fighting the lump crowding her throat. "It's only been a week."

Dory started fussing. Dave jiggled her up and down.

Jenny reached for her purse. "She needs that clove oil. I won't be gone but a minute."

"Is she hungry?"

"No, just fussy. I'm taking good care of her, Dave. I may not have your experience—"

"Or need my help."

"I told you I was sorry." She waited for him to say he accepted the apology. And waited. And waited.

Dogs and babies could sure put a kink in a mutual attraction. "But I am Dory's guardian, not you."

When he shot her an annoyed look, she backed up and tried again. "I may not do everything right, but Dory's thriving—"

"Which is more than I can say for you." He laughed. "I know what the dark circles under your eyes are, but I haven't identified the green spots on your shirt."

Warmth flooded her cheeks. She was a mess, especially next to Mr. Perfect in his navy blue pressed Dockers and pale blue Polo shirt, clean-shaven, every hair perfect. "It's spinach. Dory doesn't like spinach."

"Ah, a woman after my own heart." Dave lifted Dory over his shoulder and patted her. "I think a change of subject is in order. Did you call Loyal?"

She looked blank. "No."

He looked annoyed. "I told him you would."

"Well..."

Well, really. *Who died and made me your secretary?* She had to look at the building with him, give her approval and now call the Realtor and set up his contract? Wasn't that a little much?

"I haven't called Loyal, but I can, I guess."

He lifted a brow. "Don't you think you should?"

Certainly. What else do I have to do? He had as much time as she did, but she wasn't going to argue. If calling Loyal speeded up his moving process, then she'd do it. After she called Loyal, she'd call Mark and tell him she'd be faxing the financial report to him soon. Then she'd contact Mr. Linstrom at Rockfield Corporation and tell him that she definitely wanted to expand when Dave vacated his space. She'd rent Dave's side of the building, have the wall knocked out, new tile installed and order four additional display cases.

"I'll call Loyal when I get back." If she didn't need his space so cotton-pickin' bad, she'd tell him to do it himself.

Though she tried her best, it was late that afternoon before she found a spare minute to make the call. "Loyal? Jenny McNeill."

"Well, hello. I was beginning to think there was a problem."

"Oh, no. The building is fine."

"Well, I have the contract all ready. All you'll need to do is sign."

"Thanks. I'll tell Dave."

"There's just a few minor details. How long do you want the lease?"

"I don't know. You'll have to talk to Dave about that."

"Oh? He said to ask you."

"Me?" She dumped sugar in a kettle, then wiped Dory's mouth.

"That's what he said."

She felt uncomfortable making this kind of decision for him. "I really don't know—"

"The standard is five years. I suppose I could talk to the owner and see if he would be open to a shorter—"

"No, I'm sure the standard will be acceptable."

He'd need at least five years in the new location to get established. "I'll have Dave get back to you."

"Well, I'll need to hear from him soon."

"I'll tell him."

She hung up.

THE CLOVE OIL did the trick. That night Dory fell fast asleep in Jenny's arms after only a few minutes of rocking. Jenny was exhausted and wished she had someone to rock her to sleep. She was afraid to lay the baby down for fear she'd wake, so with one hand she pulled tax records from a box she had retrieved from the attic. She made two piles, pertinent and non-pertinent. She could kick herself for not keeping her records in one place. Some were in the attic, some in the basement and some who knew where? Once she had more space, she'd set up an office and really get organized. A notion long overdue.

Dory stirred and made sucking noises. Jenny kissed her on the head and rocked harder, thinking nothing was sweeter than a sleeping baby.

Her reverie was interrupted by the ringing telephone. She grabbed it up quickly before it woke Dory. "Hello," she said in a whisper.

"Jenny? I don't feel so good."

"Mrs. Wilcox?"

"I won't be able to work the remainder of the week. I think I've come down with something."

Sweetitis. Four pounds of fudgeballs is a lot of sugar. "I hope it's nothing serious." Jenny tried not to panic.

"I hate to leave you in a bind—"

"Don't worry about it, Mrs. Wilcox." *Stressed out is starting to feel like second nature.* "You just get well."

Hanging up, she sighed. Back to square one. But at least she'd salvaged enough fudge from Mrs. Wilcox to fill the order for the debutante ball.

TWO WEEKS PASSED, two weeks of no word from Rob and Teensy.

"Mrs. Levitt?" Jenny asked over the phone, choosing her words carefully. Rob's parents were older and in frail health. She didn't want to upset them, but she couldn't let the situation go on. "Hi. This is Jenny McNeill, owner of Fudgeballs."

"Why, yes, dear, Rob's boss."

"Would Rob happen to be there?"

"Here?" Concern flared in the woman's voice. "Why, no. Isn't he there with you?"

"No." Jenny kept her tone casual. "He and Teensy took a few days off. I thought perhaps they'd decided to visit you. There's a problem at the store I needed to talk to Rob about."

A small one, about eight months old. Teething.

"No, I haven't seen them, dear, but if I do, I'll have Robert call you immediately."

"Thank you, Mrs. Levitt." Jenny hung up, releasing a pent-up breath. Where were they? If she didn't get the financial report on Mark's desk this week, she could forget the expansion. Rockfield wouldn't hold the space vacant forever, not on Mackinac Island.

She dialed a Chicago area code and number. The phone rang twice.

"Rockfield Corporation"

"Hank Linstrom, please."

"One moment."

A woman answered on the third ring. "Mr. Linstrom, please. Jenny McNeill of Fudgeballs calling."

"I'm sorry, Ms. McNeill. Mr. Linstrom is no longer employed with Rockfield."

Jenny frowned. Hank was gone? He hadn't mentioned a word about changing jobs. She thought. Hank was the only one familiar with her particular situation. Now what?

The woman cleared her throat. "Perhaps I can help you?"

"Yes... It's about the building I'm leasing from Rockfield. There's going to be a vacancy on the other side, and I was calling to tell Hank that I definitely want the kite shop space when the tenant moves out."

The woman was overly pleasant. "I'm only a temp, but I can take a message and see that the new head of the leasing department gets it," she offered.

"Thanks. It's Jenny McNeill, with Fudgeballs. On Mackinac Island. Please make a memo that I want the space to enlarge my business."

Jenny stirred fudge as the woman carefully wrote down the information. Nearby, Dory sat in her playpen, chewing on the sleeve of her jumpsuit. Jenny waved at the baby, and Dory rewarded her with a wet, drooling grin.

"I'll make certain the proper person gets the message," the voice on the other end of the line assured her.

"Thanks." Hanging up, she glanced out the window at the dogs. Jake was digging in the flower box again. Chunks of dirt and marigolds littered the front walk. Tourists had to sidestep the messy debris as they entered the shop.

"Jake!" she bellowed.

The bulldog lifted his head, paw in midair.

She pointed her finger at him. "Stop it."

The dog's hind leg wilted. He trotted around the tree, out of sight. Moments later Jenny saw bits of marigolds flying from behind the opposite side of the trunk.

A couple of tour groups descended on the store. Luckily Mrs. Wilcox had recovered nicely from her fudge overdose and was able to help out again. The older woman waddled between the register and the candy case, working to fill orders.

It was after one o'clock before Jenny took Dory in the back room to feed her. Spooning strained carrots into the baby's mouth, she whispered, "Where *are* your mommy and daddy?" Now that Dave was actually moving, she had a zillion things to do, but first and foremost was the financial report.

When Dory fretted, Jenny sighed. "I know, I feel the same way."

Two weeks. How much longer could she keep Dory's abandonment quiet? She despised the word *abandonment*, but maybe Dave was right. Maybe Rob wasn't coming back. Panic seized her. Already well-meaning friends and business associates were starting to ask questions. How long did Rob and Teensy plan to be gone? When was Rob coming back to work? Questions she couldn't answer. She'd started ducking in the back room when Officer Jim Harris came into the store. He never failed to ask about Rob. How could she continue to explain his disappearance without Jim getting suspicious about Dory?

Carrying Dory to the front of the store, she paused, infuriated when she saw Jake nosing around Princess. Long, wet slobbers hung out of the bulldog's mouth.

She put Dory in her playpen and reached for a box of baby wipes.

JAKE SAW JENNY come out the front door, baby wipes in hand. When she advanced in his direction, he whined, backing up.

With a firm grip on his collar, she wiped his face soundly, yanking his head back and forth, making him look like a fool.

"There. Now stay away from Princess." Picking up the box of wipes, she went into the shop.

After she left, he stood, head down, humiliated. He refused to look up. He held his breath, knowing if he opened his mouth, he'd slobber again.

Hell. He couldn't help it. He was a dog, for cripe's sake.

The air whooshed out of his lungs, and he took a few panting breaths. His gaze dropped to his chest.

Damn.

Slobbers.

DURING THE AFTERNOON, Jenny kept an eye trained on Jake. Where was Dave? Couldn't he control his dog? Just once?

When she saw Jake walk over to Princess and lick

her, she saw red. Strings of long, wet drool dribbled from his mouth.

Princess shied away, whining.

"That does it." Jenny tossed a spoon aside and marched into the back room. Dory broke into a full-blown scream at the sudden commotion.

Mrs. Wilcox pinched off a bite of vanilla fudge. "Something I can help with, dear?"

"I'm looking for an extra bib!"

Pinching off a bigger hunk of fudge, Mrs. Wilcox shrugged. "All this fuss over a pooch."

Jenny walked through the store, untying the strings on one of Dory's old bibs. Outrage flooded her.

Mrs. Wilcox glanced up. "You gonna tie that on that bulldog?"

"I am. I don't have time to give Princess a bath!" She sailed out the front door as Mrs. Wilcox bit into the candy.

THE DOG'S HEAD snapped up as Jenny approached. He ran in circles around the tree until he had no chain left, then gave a low growl and bared his teeth. Undaunted, Jenny had the bib tied around his neck in two seconds flat.

He wasn't as intimidating as he thought—all bark and no bite. She'd teach him a lesson, as well as his owner.

"What do you think you're doing!" Dave burst out of Flying High, waving his broom.

Jenny straightened and met him head-on. A shouting match erupted, and Princess ran for cover with a loud yelp. A group of elderly women paused to watch the fracas, but Jenny didn't care.

"Don't ever tie a bib on my dog!"

"I'll tie a sheet on him if he keeps slobbering on Princess!"

"Dogs slobber, for crying out loud!" Dave shouted over the din.

"Not mine!" She crossed her arms over her chest.

"Oh, no, your dog never does anything—it's always Jake!"

She glared at him. "So glad you agree!"

Jenny marched into the store, so angry she couldn't speak coherently. She sputtered and shook her fist, mumbling. The man was impossible! Infuriating! Maddening!

And so incredibly handsome she wondered if she'd lost her mind, allowing two dogs to come between a budding relationship. They could be discussing dinner plans, a movie, moonlight carriage rides! Now that he was moving, the friction between them should be over. They were free to explore a mutual attraction. And she *was* attracted to him. Instead, they'd stood in the middle the street, shouting at each other like fishwives.

Jake howled and tried to paw his way out of the bib.

What was she doing, throwing the opportunity for a developing relationship down the drain? They had connected the night they looked at the new space. She'd felt it, and so did he. She'd seen it in his eyes, heard it in his voice. He was going out of his way to move in order for her to expand. She should be ashamed of treating his dog so bad.

Be adult, Jenny. Don't throw this away.

Taking a deep breath, she reined in her emotions. What was it her grandmother used to say? Why cut off her nose to spite her face?

She stuck her head out the door and shouted, "Dave?"

He glanced up. "What!"

"Coffee tonight? Seven?"

He scooped Jake up, removed the bib and angrily cast it aside.

"Well?" she demanded.

"Make it dinner. My treat!"

"Fine!"

"Fine!"

Jenny walked into the shop and slammed the screen door.

Well. She expelled a breath of relief. *We have a date tonight.*

6

"GOOD NEWS and bad news," Sam Freeman announced. "Which do you want to hear first?"

Dave tapped his pencil against the side of his half-empty coffee mug, daring to hope the private detective had found his daughter. The last thing he wanted was bad news this early in the afternoon. "Give me the good. Did you find them?"

"Yeah, I found them."

"Good." Dave sat up straighter. "When will Megan be here?"

Sam cleared his throat. "That's the bad news. They're due back the first of September."

"What do you mean, due back? Didn't you remind Nancy this is my month to have Megan?"

"Didn't get to talk to Nancy personally. Tried to get word to her, but they're not accepting phone calls or messages."

Dave let out his breath loudly. *"They?"*

"More bad news. Nancy got married in France and is honeymooning on a private yacht. The happy couple has more security than Bill Clinton."

Dave felt sick. His chances of having Megan during August were slipping through his fingers. "For crying out loud, who the hell did she marry? Jonathan Pharis the Third?''

"How'd you know?''

"How'd I know what?''

"She married Jonathan Pharis the Third.''

"You're kidding.''

"'Fraid not.''

"Jonathan Pharis—the shipping magnate?''

"The same.''

Dave threw the pencil across the room. It bounced off an alien face and fell to the floor. "Where's my daughter?''

"On the ship with them. Like I said, I tried to get—''

"Trying's not good enough, Freeman. I don't care what you have to do, you get my kid off that damn boat and back here now!''

Dave banged the receiver down and paced the small cubicle he called an office. He impatiently ran his fingers through his hair and down the back of his neck. A headache throbbed at the base of his skull—a headache by the name of Nancy. He knew Nancy and could predict the future. She'd travel all over the world and drag Megan with her. Hell, she'd probably *move* to France. Damn her! He'd rot in hell before he'd let her keep Megan away from him. He didn't care how much money Jonathan Pharis the Third had. Jonathan Pharis the Third wasn't going to have Dave's daughter.

Glancing out the window, Dave felt the hackles on his neck rise. Jenny had walked out of the shop with a bowl of fresh water for Princess. Jake had backed off, giving her plenty of leeway.

A bib. Dave snorted. That woman was going to make his dog paranoid.

"WOMEN!" Jake growled as Jenny left. He curled his upper lip over his teeth. "Put that damn bib on me again, human, and you and me..." He trailed off in a rambling spurt of disjointed mumblings.

Princess strutted back and forth, refusing to look at him. "Men!"

She was really starting to get to him. The broad was hyper. Keeping an eye on her, he tried to sneak a chew of his bone, but she strutted back and he had to quickly roll over to hide his treasure. He stuck all four legs in the air.

Wrinkling her nose with disgust, she turned away. "How crude. Have you no decency?"

Maybe she'll go away if I don't answer.

She whirled. "Get up! You look like an imbecile lying that way!"

"I can lay any way I want. This is my side of the tree."

"Get up, I say, before someone sees you and hauls you off!"

"I'm not moving. I'm comfortable." Actually, the bone was killing him, jabbing in his back. He wished she'd move on so he could get up.

Princess sniffed. "You have the decorum of a warthog!"

That does it! He sprang to his feet and lunged toward her.

She sprinted just beyond his reach.

Bouncing on his hind legs, he felt his collar slip off.

Free at last!

His eyes narrowed. "Now you've had it, you little French twister."

She let out an earsplitting yip that curled his hair. "Hey, calm down, calm down!" He pinned her to the ground with a paw as her spindly legs flailed the air wildly. "You'll have the humans down on us!"

True to his words, the fudge shop door sprang open, and Jenny rushed out with a broom in her hand.

Hoo, boy.

"Get away!" she yelled, menacing him with the broom.

He had Frenchie down, and he wasn't letting her up unless the human went for that hose again. He eyed Jenny, keeping a firm paw on the Brillo pad.

"Let me up, you big bébé!" Princess yelped.

Jake glanced down, grinning. "Make me."

He saw stars as the broom landed against the flat of his butt.

"Hey!"

Jake shook his head, trying to focus as he heard the squeal of brakes and Officer Jim Harris waded into the melee. In disbelief Jake watched as the man took a hook from the back of his bike. He threw a dogcatcher's ring around Jake's neck and dragged him to the cage on the back of the vehicle.

Jenny ran after the officer, waving a chocolate-stained spoon. "That's not necessary, Jim!" she called over the yelping and howling.

Jim, struggling to get Jake in the cage and the door closed, yelled over his shoulder, "I can't hear you! Call me later!"

"But Jim!" she hollered as he gave her a friendly salute and drove away.

She glanced at the kite shop, then stepped back, cradling Princess protectively to her breast. Dave suddenly loomed in his doorway, his face a thundercloud. His gaze followed Jake down the street, imprisoned in the small cage.

Jake stared at him pitifully.

Meeting Dave's glower, Jenny hugged Princess tighter, muffling her dog's cries. "Don't look at me. I tried to stop him—"

"If I hear 'I tried' one more time today—"

When she opened her mouth to explain, he lifted his hand, palm outward, his features cold.

"Just tell me where to pick up my dog."

"Dave, I didn't mean for your dog—"

His glacial stare stopped her. "*Where* can I get Jake?"

"The island pound," she answered, making her response deliberately curt. She sighed. "Take your checkbook. It'll cost you."

"That's just *great*." He stepped into the kite shop and slammed the door.

She blinked, staring at the closed door, wondering if it meant their date for tonight was off.

"Men!" she scoffed.

Princess snuggled closer. "Yip!" *Ditto!*

DAVE ARRIVED at Jenny's at ten to seven lugging two sacks of groceries.

"What's all this?" she asked, surprised but delighted he'd decided to show up. "I thought you'd pick up a pizza or something."

"Pizza!" Dave pretended to be repelled by the idea. "Springing a dog from the Big House makes a man hungry."

She laughed. "I'm glad you came, and relieved to see you still have a sense of humor."

"I fail to see anything funny about Jake being hauled off to the pound."

She followed him into the kitchen and he ceremoniously unpacked the bags and placed cans and spices on the counter.

"You're not mad?"

"I'm not mad. Moreover, you will think you've died and gone to heaven once you've tasted Spaghetti Kasada."

"Hm, I will, will I?" She examined a couple of the spices. "You really have a thing for Italian food, don't you?"

He rescued the vials from her hand. "Don't be nosing around for my secrets." He smiled, his gaze resting on her soft features. "You look tired."

"Awful's a better word." She touched her hair. "I had a time getting Dory to sleep. She likes to play with my hair while I rock her."

Who wouldn't, he thought, eyeing the thick blond mane pulled into a jaunty ponytail. "You don't look awful, you look like a woman with a busy life. Actually, you look...nice." She looked more than nice. She looked like someone he'd like to wake up next to every morning. Soft, warm... He shook the thought aside and turned his attention to his culinary efforts. "Got a big pot?"

She pushed away from the counter and knelt to get the pan from a lower cabinet. He reached and stopped her. He was right. She was soft and warm. "I'll get it."

When she straightened, her face was so close he could smell her perfume. When was the last time he wanted a woman, needed one? Ached for one? Hell, when was the last time he was this close to one alone?

He stepped back. "Why don't you relax in the living room and let your personal chef do his thing."

She smiled. "Thank you, kind sir. You'll find everything you need in the top cabinet."

"Thanks." *Back off, Dave*, he thought. He was glad she left the room. There was no way he could concentrate on cooking when all he could do was admire the way she filled out a pair of jeans and the cleavage he saw in the V of her pink cotton knit top. "Stick to cooking," he mumbled as he searched for a spoon.

Twenty minutes later, the sauce simmering, he walked into the living room and found Jenny curled up on the couch sound asleep. Her head was squeezed between the armrest and a cushion, and she looked uncomfortable as hell. He put his hand under her head and tried to place a pillow there, but she roused and sat up.

"I'm sure good company, huh?" she said, yawning.

"Here." He lowered himself to the couch and eased her back to him. "You look like you could use a little down time." His thumbs gently kneaded the knots in her shoulders. "Relax."

Sounds emanated from her throat like tiny mews. "Mmm, that feels good."

Yes, it certainly did, he decided, pulling her closer while the heels of his palms pressed circles on her upper arms. He took a deep breath and savored her delicate scent. It wasn't overpowering, like Nancy's perfume. But it was intoxicating.

A few moments of massage, and he knew he'd better get up while he could. Simply being with her aroused him. Touching her tempted him to do so much more. He guided her shoulders against the couch, stood and put a throw pillow on top of the coffee table.

"What are you doing?" she asked.

"Making madam comfortable. What's all this?" he asked, moving aside a stack of receipts strewn on the table.

"My tax records. I have to get a financial report together—"

"Not tonight, you don't. Tonight you relax."

He slipped her sneakers off and placed her bare feet on the cushion. Even her feet inspired ideas he shouldn't have, but feet were safer than thinking about her breasts. It was already too late to keep from getting aroused.

She smiled, pulling her foot away when he began rubbing the bottom. "That tickles."

"Just hold still. Apparently I'm not pressing hard enough."

His thumbs circled the pad of her foot while his

fingers massaged the top. He felt her relax and her leg go limp.

She leaned back and closed her eyes. "Mmm. Spaghetti Kasada *and* a foot rub. What did I do to deserve this?"

He grinned as contentment spread over her face. He pulled her foot close against him and massaged her ankle and up her calf. Her warmth was contagious. So was she, he realized. He'd be more than happy to let dinner burn if he could take her in his arms and—

The tightening in his groin was painful. He was wrong. Feet weren't safe enough.

"How's Jake?"

"A little testy, but I gave him a T-bone steak before I left. He seemed in a better mood."

"I am sorry about the incident this afternoon, but it really wasn't my fault."

"I know." He massaged the foot, admiring her polish. "I like the shade. What's it called?"

"I have no idea," Jenny murmured, stretching lazily. "Something I picked up at the salon."

The cloth of her T-shirt tightened over her breasts. His gaze was riveted to the seductive sight, and he realized the massage was a bad idea, period.

He eased her foot to the cushion and released it, but her eyes snapped open, making his escape harder than he thought. "I think the sauce is burning."

"Need help?"

A lot of it. "No, stay where you are."

FULL OF SPAGHETTI, cheese bread and salad, they convened to the couch around nine.

Jenny covered her stomach with her hands and moaned. "I ate too much."

Settling back, Dave stretched out. "I'm glad you liked it. I enjoy cooking."

He could feel her studying him. What was she thinking? Was she wondering why he wasn't still married? Good question. David knew he was solid, dependable, a smart businessman, he'd like to think a good father. Was she wondering what happened to break up his marriage? Was it him, was it her?

"You don't seem the domestic type. I had you figured for a man who eats at the finest restaurants, has dinner parties catered—"

"That's how it was when Nancy and I were married," he admitted. "She never cooked, and I didn't know how, but after the divorce, I discovered the joys of eating at home."

"Oh? That's a joy?" She laughed.

"I think so. During a blue funk period, I was lying on the couch, watching a chef on Oprah, and I thought, 'I can do that.'"

"No kidding? One episode of Oprah, and you became a chef?"

"Just like that." He snapped his fingers. "What about you? I'll bet you can whip up a mean meal."

She shook her head. "Not really. Fudge is my specialty. In a pinch, I can throw a few things together out of a can and make a passable casserole. I'm mostly a breakfast person."

"Omelets? Eggs Benedict?"

"Cornflakes."

They burst out laughing. Their amusement disturbed Dory, and Jenny went to the bedroom and brought her out.

"Look who's here." She pointed toward Dave. "Wave to Uncle Dave." She picked up Dory's arm and wagged it back and forth. When the baby spotted Dave, she grinned and reached for him.

"Ah, women," Dave sighed, "they can't leave me alone."

Jenny made a face and handed Dory to him. "That's understandable. You have your moments."

Cradling the baby in the crook of his arm, he tickled her under her chin. "You ever think about having kids of your own?"

Jenny sank down on the sofa beside him, leaning close to look at Dory's new teeth. Her bare arm brushed his. "I've thought about it, especially when I was with Brian. Maybe someday. Right now I'm too busy to think about it."

"The expansion?"

She nodded. "What's the old saying? When opportunity knocks, open the door."

"Strike while the iron's hot," he agreed, thinking she couldn't have struck at a more opportune time. It was a sheer stroke of luck that she'd decided to move without being forced. She was going to be upset enough when he got around to telling her he owned the building.

She tickled Dory under the chin and made her laugh. "Something like that."

"Don't wait too long." He watched her eyes light up as she played with the baby. "Having a child is the greatest thing that can happen to you."

She smiled. "Heard anything about your daughter?"

He wasn't going to bring that up. He'd come here to have a quiet dinner with a friend, but he'd be lying if he said Sam Freeman's phone call hadn't been on his mind all evening. Now that he was holding a baby in his arms, and all he could think about was Megan.

"I got word today. Nancy remarried and they're due back from their honeymoon the first part of September." When he glanced at her he was surprised to see her eyes were misty.

"Couldn't you have Megan flown home earlier?"

"I would if I could talk to her—or Nancy." He felt his anger surface. "I have a few choice words I'd like to say to Nancy—like, what in the hell runs through your brain, dragging Megan all over Europe, cavorting with God only knows who?"

"Dave." She laid her hand over his. "I'm sure your ex-wife wouldn't do anything to jeopardize the well-being of your daughter. After all, Megan is her child, too."

He held his breath, along with more angry words. She was right. Just the thought of Nancy set him on edge. Lifting Dory to his shoulder, he gently burped her. "Sorry—it's just so damn frustrating. I don't care that Nancy's married one of the richest men in France. All I can think about is Megan being hauled around the world, living a life I know she hates. Megan likes to sleep in the same bed every night. She craves security."

She leaned back and rested her head against the sofa as she gazed at him. He wondered if that look meant she would be receptive to a kiss. Was she willing to see him as more than a helpful neighbor? Had Brian caused her to shy away from all men?

"Life stinks sometimes." She took a deep breath. "I thought my life was over when it finally dawned on me that Brian was never going to commit to marriage. I had planned for seven years to settle down with him, have a bunch of kids and live happily ever after." She sighed. "But, if it's any consolation, things have a way of working out. They did for me, anyway. What is it they say? God closes one door and opens another? Now things are going so well with Fudgeballs that I don't have time for marriage, children or happily ever after."

He admired her outlook on life. Her eyes shone with promise of a brighter tomorrow, and he found himself wishing he had her faith. How he wished... Leaning over, he put his hand to her cheek and started to pull her closer when she whispered, "You're beeping."

"Huh?"

"That beeping—either it's my microwave or you're being summoned."

He groaned and reached for the pager on his belt. Glancing at the number, he frowned. "Sorry. It's Freeman. I need to return his call." He handed Dory to her.

"Sure." She pointed toward the kitchen.

He found the phone on the kitchen wall. "Sam? Dave Kasada." He braced himself against the kitchen counter.

"Dave, there's someone here who wants to talk to you."

"Daddy?"

"Sweetheart?" Dave held his hand over the phone and called out to Jenny. "It's Megan!"

Jenny smiled at him through the open doorway and gave him a thumbs-up.

"Daddy, I miss you."

He wanted to crawl into the phone and hug her. It had been weeks since he'd heard her voice. "Hey, Meggie, I've missed you, too. Where are you, honey?"

"On a big boat. That friend of yours, Mr. Freeman? Well, he rowed out here and told Mommy you wanted to talk to me."

"I do. I've been looking all over for you."

"You have?"

"I sure have." He wanted more than this. Now that he had his daughter on the phone and was assured she was safe and sound, he wanted Nancy's hide. "I miss you—I want you to come stay with me."

"I miss you too, Daddy. My new daddy..." Her voice dropped. "He's cranky sometimes. He says, 'Megan, go to your stateroom while Mommy and I talk.'" She sighed. "I have to go to my room all the time, Daddy. I don't like it. I want to play with Duffer. He lets me fish."

"Who's Duffer?"

"That nice man in the white coat that serves our dinner every night."

Dave stiffened with resentment. Pharis was sending

Megan to her room so he could— "Meggie, honey, where's Mommy?"

"Right here."

"Put her on."

"Okay. Mommy says she wants to talk to you, too. I love you, Daddy."

"Love you, too, sweetheart." His lips thinned. They sent her to the stateroom early every night? "Yes, Nancy, I'm here. Where the hell did you think I'd be? I've been waiting to hear from you. It's August. Do I have to remind you that August is *my* month to have Megan?"

"Sorry, David—with the chaos of wedding arrangements and the— You just wouldn't believe what we've been through, and now your Mr. Freeman shows up right in the middle of cocktails—"

"Cut to the chase, Nancy. I don't care about your chaos or your cocktails. I want Megan before school starts."

"Dave, we need to talk about Megan's custody. Now that I'm married, I'll be traveling more, and Jonathan says—" She stopped abruptly. "This is hardly the time or the place to discuss this. I'll call you when I get back to the States."

"And when might that be?"

"Sometime after Labor Day."

A muscle twitched in his jaw. "What about my time with Megan, Nancy? I have visitation rights and—"

"I said I was sorry. I have to go. We'll talk later." The line went dead.

He held the phone out, gritting his teeth, staring at it for a long moment before hanging up. "*Damn* her."

"Trouble?" Jenny walked into the kitchen carrying Dory.

The baby reached for him, and he took her and held her tightly to his chest. "Nancy wants to talk to me about Megan's custody."

Jenny took a glass from the cabinet and turned on the tap. "What about it?"

"I don't know. That's the problem." His features sobered. "If she thinks she's going to keep Megan from me, she's got another think coming. I'll fight her with every cent I have."

"Dave." Jenny touched his arm lightly. "Don't borrow trouble."

She drank the glass of water and turned out the light as they left the kitchen. Settling onto the sofa, Dave held Dory as Jenny readied the baby for bed.

The genuine concern in her eyes affected him. Why couldn't Nancy have some of her compassion? Without thinking, he reached over and slipped his free arm around her neck, pulling her to him. He needed her and her strength. The gentle warmth of her breath fanned his lips.

"Don't borrow trouble," she repeated, and they both knew she was talking about something entirely different this time.

Princess suddenly woke from a dead sleep, sprang to his lap, sniffed Dory, then licked him on the cheek.

He drew back and wiped his face on his sleeve. It wasn't the kiss he'd anticipated. No wonder the dog got on his nerves. Checking his watch, he realized he'd overstayed his welcome. "It's late. I need to be going."

Jenny got up to walk him to the door. "Did you call Loyal about the lease?"

Frowning, he kissed Dory good-night, then handed her over. "I thought you did that."

"I called him, but I wasn't sure about the length of the lease. I said you'd call him." She adjusted the baby's lightweight blanket.

"Me?" He frowned. "Yeah, I can call him. What sort of lease did he offer?"

"The standard five years."

"That would be all right, wouldn't it?"

"It would be for me."

"Okay, I'll call him first thing in the morning and tell him to draw up a five-year lease." He'd thought she was decisive. She seemed in control. Why was she leaving something as important as a lease up to him? Still, since she was inadvertently doing him a favor, he couldn't complain.

Pausing at the door, he thought about kissing her good-night but decided not to push his luck. Two aborted attempts didn't bode well. The night had been enjoyable, easy, no pressure. Why not keep it that way?

"Good night," she whispered.

"Good night."

As the door closed, he suddenly wished he wasn't so prudent. What would a kiss have hurt?

"Loyal, draw up the standard lease on that floor space." Through the window, Dave watched Jake wrestle with Princess. "Oh, yes, she wants it—I don't know why she's dragging her feet. Might be she doesn't have her finances in order. I do know she's been working on her books a lot lately— Jake! Get away from her!"

Dave tapped on the window. "I gotta go, Loyal. Dog trouble again. Just put a hold on the property. If you need earnest money, I'll send you a check myself. I can't get away this afternoon, but I'll drop it in the mail and collect from Jenny later."

He hung up, stepped outside and walked to where Jake was tied. "Good boy," he said as he untangled the chain from the tree and gave him a dog bone. Jake thanked him by licking his hand. Dave patted him on the head. "Learn to leave the woman alone, and you'll have it made."

Princess strutted around her area. "You stop vamping Jake," Dave warned her, shaking his finger at her. He grinned when she licked his hand. *Women.*

"Problems?" Jenny called from the door of her shop.

Dave turned and smiled. "Just trying to prevent some," he said, walking toward her. "Hi."

"Hi."

"How are you and Dory today?"

"We *both* slept like babies last night. Except for overindulging in Spaghetti Kasada, I'm great."

His gaze skimmed her tanned legs encased in white shorts. "I can see that. What are you doing for lunch?"

"Lunch!" She laughed. "What's lunch? I can't remember the last time I took a lunch break."

"Then it's high time you started. I thought Dory might enjoy an outing. Want to grab an ice-cream cone?"

She looked as if she wanted to accept.

"I don't know, Dave. It's been pretty hectic around here this morning."

"Come on. Mrs. Wilcox can handle things for an hour, and Peter could use an extra hour's pay. Let's do something crazy."

She shrugged, grinning. "Why not? Give me a sec to get the baby."

"Don't forget the diaper bag," he called to her retreating back.

"Did you call Loyal?"

"Called him." It was settled. She was locked into a five-year lease.

"OOH, DORY! Look at the pretty kite." Jenny pointed to the sky, and Dory squealed with delight. "Oops! Watch it, Uncle Dave! You nearly lost it."

"Never! I'm a champion kite master. You want to take over?" He ran a short way along the shoreline, then backed up, pulling the kite in all directions.

"No." She settled on the blanket and yawned. "Looks too much like exercise to me. I try to avoid that sort of thing." She pulled Dory's bonnet over the baby's head. Dory immediately yanked it off with a fussy squeal. What was she doing here? She had hours of work piled up, and poor Mrs. Wilcox would be inundated. She smiled at Dave trotting along the shoreline, flying the Alien.

"We want ice cream, Dave," she called.

He nodded and began winding the kite string in. "In a minute!"

When he returned, she was sitting cross-legged on the blanket in front of Dory, studying the baby's tiny fingers.

"Hello, ladies. Miss me?"

"Something terrible."

Dropping on the blanket beside her, he gazed at Dory. "What are the two of you doing? Complaining about men?"

"Certainly not. We like men, don't we, Dory? I was just marveling over her perfect little fingernails, all rounded on the ends. "

"You'll have to get her to give you the name of her nail tech."

Jenny grinned. "Babies are truly God's miracles."

She watched him roll to his back and stare at the flawless blue sky, thankful that he seemed relaxed and at peace with the world. The picnic had done him a world of good. She was glad she had agreed to come along.

"Want another piece of chicken?"

"No, thanks." She redid her ponytail, aware of his eyes on her. Was he interested in a relationship? Was it too soon for him? Did memories of one failed marriage color his perspective of another? She wrapped the band around her hair and formed a tight knot. "We want ice cream, huh, Dory?"

The baby bucked and grinned.

Ten minutes later he returned with three drippy cones. "Okay, sports fans, here it is."

"It's about time," she teased. "*I* was about to start whining."

A few short weeks ago, sitting on a blanket and eating ice cream with a man and a baby was the farthest thing from her mind. Yet here they were, lapping up strawberry ice cream as if they hadn't a care in the world.

Leaning on one elbow, she watched Dave spoon-feed Dory, more melting down her chin than down her throat. Licking her cone, she was reminded that this could have been her and Brian with their child. Brian. Suddenly she had trouble making the picture fit. No, Brian wouldn't be spoon-feeding a baby. Brian would be off doing his own thing. He'd never had time for children. She always felt that would change once they married, but she knew now what a foolish concept that was. Children were high maintenance.

Laughing, Dave glanced at her. "She loves this stuff. I can't shovel it in fast enough."

Jenny pulled a baby wipe from the box and made a couple of swipes at Dory's mouth, then put the baby's sun bonnet in place. Dory twisted her head sideways and jerked the bonnet off again.

"Oh, Mom," Dave mocked, "quit it. What's a little sunburn between friends?"

She glanced up. "What'd you call me?"

"Mom— Sorry, I was only kidding."

"No, I liked it. Mom." She thought about it. "Yeah, has a nice ring to it, don't you think?"

Dave spooned more ice cream into Dory's open mouth. "I'm sorry I said you weren't qualified to care for a child. The way you've been with Dory, I think you'd make a wonderful mom.''

She slapped her hand over her heart, mocking a near faint. ''Dave Kasada thinks I'd make a good mom?''

He slung a spoonful of ice cream at her. It landed on her cheek and slid down the neck of her blouse.

''Why, you…'' She took what was left of her cone and smeared it across his face.

He grabbed her arm and wrestled her to the blanket, leaning down to wipe his gooey face against hers. They had a friendly wrestling match before he pinned her, their lips only a breath apart. She could feel every contour of his body molded against hers and she liked it. Far too much. Dormant feelings suddenly sprang to life and frightened her.

''Jenny—''

Her mind protested the kiss that was about to take place, but her body and soul met the challenge eagerly. She felt his breath warm her cheek just before his lips closed over hers. Like in an old movie, music played, drums rolled, bombs exploded and a million bright lights flickered a myriad of colors.

A long moment later, he pulled back and gazed into her eyes. ''What the hell was that?''

She closed her eyes, plagued with the sinking feeling she knew exactly what it was. She was falling in love—or something pretty darn close.

In thirty-one years, she had never felt like this with a man. Breathless, giddy, wildly irrational. Dangerous territory. Involvement with him would only complicate her life. Besides, she knew nothing about him except he was a kite maker, a good father, antimarriage and possessed looks and charm that could make a grown woman cry. She had to get a grip. Dave was the first honest man she'd met. He shot straight from the hip, and she should do no less with him. She had to pull back, retreat before it was too late.

She rolled from beneath him and sat up. "It's getting late. I need to get back."

Disappointment crossed his face, but he complied.

As she tried to tie Dory's bonnet on, he caught her wrist. "I'm sorry if I offended you."

"You didn't." She laughed, afraid she'd cry. "One kiss—big deal." On top of everything else, she was becoming a gifted liar. It *was* a big deal. She wasn't sure she could even stand up.

He began gathering Dory's toys and stuffing them in the diaper bag. "How about a real date some night? Dinner. Name your favorite restaurant."

"I don't think so."

"Why not?"

"People will talk."

"So what? We're of age."

"No, I mean *talk* talk. They'll have us sleeping together and picking out our silverware pattern. You know how people are. Nothing against you personally, I just don't have time right now for a relationship." She picked Dory up and kissed her on the cheek.

She could lie with the best of them.

7

"WANT TO HEAR a funny joke?" Dave asked.

"How crude is it?" Jenny replied.

"It's not crude—it's dumb."

"What?"

"Haven't you ever heard a dumb joke?"

"How dumb?"

"There was this guy and his dog watching a movie, and the dog was laughing so hard tears were rolling down his cheeks. A man next to them said, 'Is that your *dog* laughing?' The man said, 'Yes, and I don't understand it. He *hated* the book.'"

Jenny looked at him strangely. "Well, that answered my question. *Extremely* dumb." She groaned as they walked into Fudgeballs. "I can't believe you think that's funny."

"I didn't say I thought it was funny. I asked if you wanted to hear it. Want to hear another one?"

"Not today. One's enough." She laughed. She and Dave had had such a good time together. She was glad to have him as a friend and wasn't going to wish for anything more.

Dory was nodding on Dave's shoulder, her tiny arm draped around his neck. The tip of her nose was pink from the fresh air and sunshine.

Jenny's smile faded when she saw Rob and Teensy standing behind the glass counter. Their appearance was so unexpected she felt her legs threaten to buckle.

Rob smiled. "Hey, like, hello."

A knot formed in the pit of Jenny's stomach. For a moment she thought she was going to be sick. "Rob. Teensy," she managed to say.

"They showed up not ten minutes after you left." Mrs. Wilcox slid a pan of fudge into the display case. "I didn't know exactly where you were, or I would've sent someone to get you." Shuffling to the register, she speared receipts on a spindle.

"It's okay." Jenny motioned for Dave to set Dory in the playpen. He gently settled the sleeping infant, looking to her for a reaction. What did he expect? For her to make a scene, start bawling and say it wasn't fair for them to run off and leave the child with someone who was going to fall in love with her and not want to give her up?

That's what she wanted to do, but she kept quiet, swallowing her disappointment.

Dory belonged with her parents. Jenny had known that all along. Their return was just so sudden, so unsettling.

Teensy rushed around the counter to claim Dory. The infant raised a fuss as her mother showered her neck, face and chin with kisses. "Hi, baby. Mmm, kissee, kissee, kissee—did you miss Mommie?"

Rob joined her. The knot in Jenny's stomach tightened as she watched the display of family affection. She should be thrilled Rob and Teensy were back. Now she could get on with her plans. She wouldn't have to worry about mixing formula in the middle of the night, strained carrots on her best blouse and teething. She should be overjoyed, so why wasn't she? Instead, she felt like going on an eating binge.

Dave somberly stood aside to allow the parents access to their daughter.

"Hey, Dave." Rob flashed a good-natured grin. "How's it going?"

"Good. How about you?"

With his arm around Teensy's waist, Rob gazed at her. "Awesome, man. Really awesome."

Jenny finally found her voice, trying to keep a neutral tone. "I was worried about you. You left so suddenly."

"Sorry about that." Teensy's earthy kiss severed Rob's response. The lovers engaged in a heated kiss that embarrassed Jenny. As the lip lock went on and on, she glanced at Dave, who discreetly looked the other way. Obviously, whatever problems the couple had encountered had been settled. If Dory hadn't started crying, Jenny was prepared to go for the hose and break up the passionate embrace.

"Ooh, is Mommie's wittle angel fussy?" Teensy gathered an out-of-sorts Dory in her arms, smoothing tendrils of baby hair from the infant's face. "Ooh, your nose is all pink. Have you been in the sun too long?"

Jenny looked away. "She wouldn't keep her hat on."

Customers were pouring into the shop. Jenny realized the reunion was blocking traffic. "I'll take Dory into the back room and—"

"Jenny?" Rob stopped her, his features sobering. Jenny glanced over her shoulder. "Yes?"

"We, uh, can't— We just stopped by to pick up Dory."

The knot in her stomach turned into a fist. A big, angry fist threatening to shut off her air supply.

He shrugged, his eyes offering a silent apology. "We're on our way to New York."

The news echoed like a gunshot. A hush fell over the room. Shoppers quietly selected purchases while keeping a guarded eye on the scene playing out before them. They couldn't know how the announcement would affect her, yet instinct told her they knew something was amiss.

"Oh?" Jenny tried to keep her response upbeat. "Going to spend a few days with your parents?"

"No, going there to look for work." He glanced at Teensy. "We've stayed in one place too long. It's time to move on."

The pain grew. It was his right—their right. She had no reason to feel as if she was being victimized. Six weeks ago, Dory had been just a cute baby who belonged to the couple who worked for her. Why did it suddenly feel as if her child was being threatened?

She looked to Dave for emotional support, praying he could help. He said nothing, but she could see he was warring with his emotions. They had allowed themselves to get too close, started thinking they were a family, acting like family, going on picnics and eating strawberry ice cream together. Flying kites.

Jenny automatically waited on clientele, ignoring Teensy's incessant cooing. Mrs. Wilcox had steered clear of the discussion, waiting on customers while Jenny dealt with the situation. As she weighed and counted fudgeballs, she watched Rob and Teensy move about, gathering personal belongings and stuffing them in knapsacks. Dory's bibs and diapers were packed, her two carriers and playpen folded and laid beside the other items. Teensy juggled the baby, as if unaware of the chaos they were causing.

Dave walked around the counter, and a moment later Jenny felt his hand at her hip, the soft brush of his breath against her cheek as he leaned close and whispered, "I'm next door if you need me."

"Thanks." She blinked back tears, trying to read the numbers on the scales. She didn't want to think how this would affect their relationship. From the moment Rob left, she and Dave had shared responsibility for the child. When Dory was no longer around, how often would he stop by to visit?

As he was leaving, Dave paused to tweak Dory under the chin. "So long, Munchkin."

Dory giggled, thrashing her feet.

He focused on Teensy. "She's got a tooth."

Blowing a gum bubble, Teensy's face brightened. The bubble popped. "She does?" She poked a finger in Dory's mouth, searching for proof. Dory bit her, and she jerked back, laughing. "Look, Rob. She does!"

"If you look close, you'll see the beginnings of another one," Dave encouraged.

"Two! Awesome!"

Dave stepped to the door. "Jenny took pictures—you'll want a copy before you leave."

"Cool," Rob said.

It took less than fifteen minutes for the happy couple to collect their personal belongings. "That about does it," Rob announced as he emerged from the back room. He paused, catching Teensy for another long, involved kiss.

Jenny wiped her hands on her apron and stepped to the register. She opened it and removed a check. Tapping Rob on the shoulder, she said, "You'll need this."

Rob glanced at the check as he broke off the kiss. "Thanks."

"Don't thank me. I owed you for a week's pay when you left."

Rob pocketed the check, then picked up the carriers, playpen and knapsacks. "Later, dude."

Jenny refused to look at him. "Yeah, later." She weakened, her eyes riveted on Dory as Rob smiled at Teensy and motioned her toward the door. Grinning, Teensy manipulated one of Dory's arms to wave at Jenny. She waved back, smiling though tears. "Bye, sweetie."

They disappeared though the doorway and she raced to the window to look out. The infatuated couple were holding hands, walking toward the dock to catch the two o'clock ferry.

"Life can hurt sometimes." Mrs. Wilcox approached from behind. "I lost a young 'un once. Just a few days old, but a person can still get mighty attached to a baby in a very short time."

Jenny's courage crumbled. She buried her face in

her hands and sobbed. "I knew Rob would come back—I shouldn't have let myself get so close."

"Aw." Mrs. Wilcox awkwardly patted her back. "Don't be ashamed to cry, honey. Lovin' someone ain't bad, it's not lovin' that gets you in trouble."

Soft, golden rays settled into the Mackinac Straits as day gently surrendered to evening.

Dave poured Coke into a glass of ice, then carried the drink to the flagstone patio where he pulled up a chair and propped his feet on the low stone wall to watch the sunset. The honeysuckle climbing along Aunt Mosie's lattice trellis scented the air and reminded him of Jenny. Was she as lonely tonight as he was?

A light breeze sprang up as he studied the tree line along the bluffs, thinking how complicated life had become. At one point, he'd thought he owned the world.

Without Megan, he felt empty.

Dory and Jenny had filled his empty places. For a while, he'd laughed again. Now Dory was gone. Without Dory, Jenny didn't need him. The empty places were back, deeper and darker.

Melancholy settled around his shoulders like a heavy mantle as he watched a songbird fly. What hurt more? Losing Dory or losing his reason to spend time with Jenny? The relationship had started out so innocently. When had his feelings become more substantial, more disturbing? He'd just come out of a bad marriage. The last thing he wanted was to open himself to hurt again. He'd had his fill of lawyers and shouting matches.

Dory had brought out paternal feelings, feelings he couldn't deny. Exactly where did Jenny fit in his life? Until they'd spent time together, she was merely an obstacle to overcome, a hindrance, someone who occupied space in his building that he wanted. The last few weeks, she'd become more. Tonight he was hurting for her, and he hated the feeling.

Leaning back in the wicker chair, he closed his eyes, soaking in the waning rays of sunlight. The house was so damn quiet tonight. He listened to the faint rustle of leaves, the melodic cry of the songbird, aware he'd never felt more alone. This was the hardest hour, the hour when he used to come home and play with Megan. They'd toss a ball around the yard, play jacks, his large fingers clumsy next to her tiny ones, or eat cookies and drink tea seated at her red and white table and chairs in the playroom. He bit back pain, wondering if it would get any easier. Would he ever stop waking up in the middle of the night, hearing the way her voice sounded? "Oh, Daaddy," she'd say when he razzed her about her hair or about marrying the scrawny kid down the street.

What must Jenny be feeling right now? This was the hour she'd feed Dory, take her for an evening stroll, give her a bath—

The doorbell rang, interrupting his thoughts. Wiping a hand across his face, he got up. When he opened the door, Jenny was standing before him, red-eyed.

They stood for a moment without speaking.

Tears slid from the corners of her eyes and dripped off her cheeks. Swallowing, he felt his common sense draining away. Hell. He always was a sucker for tears.

He opened his arms, and she threw herself into his embrace, her breasts pressing into his chest, her hands clinching behind his neck. "Now, now, what's all this?" he said, hugging her tighter. She glanced up and started to speak, but he silenced her with his finger.

"I understand. There's no need for words." He knew she pressed her forehead against him to hide her tears. "You don't have to be tough for me." His hand moved to her ponytail, and he removed the band, freeing the silky strands. He slipped his fingers into the golden curls and eased them to her shoulders.

"Oh, Dave, I feel so…so…"

"Empty?" He felt her nod, then shiver. "If I could take away your pain, I would. I know what empty feels like."

Jenny took a step back, wiping her eyes. "I'm so sorry."

"For what? You haven't done anything to be sorry for," he said, taking her hand in his. Tears streamed down her face, and he wanted to kiss them away. She was so very vulnerable. Tonight wasn't the time for apologies. It was a time to console. All he wanted to do was put a smile on her face.

Her voice sounded small and scared. "Until Rob and Teensy took Dory away, I could only imagine how you felt about Megan. Now I know, and what I imagined wasn't nearly as bad as this."

He pulled her into his arms and held her close as

she sobbed. Long minutes passed while she allowed her grief to show. He wanted to tell her how glad he was she had come to him to share this moment, to find solace with him. It made him feel good to know she'd come to him first.

When the tears subsided, he led her into the small den at the back of the house.

Jenny sighed, drained of emotion. He thoughtfully poured her a glass of wine and allowed her a few moments to compose herself. She should be embarrassed for bawling like a baby, but he seemed to understand. He left the cozy den to get something from his bedroom, and she wondered what was taking him so long.

She glanced at the staircase and wiped her nose when he appeared at the top, making his way toward her. He had something in his hand, something too small to see. A shiver ran down her spine when he sat next to her on the couch, his leg touching hers.

He picked up her hand and laid a small, black velvet box in her palm. "For you."

Her stomach turned to warm mush. Why did she feel as though this was prom night and he was the first date of her life? Because he excited her in a way no man ever had, and she wasn't sure how long she'd be able to conceal her feelings from him, especially when she was hurting like this.

"Open it."

The twinkle in his eyes reminded her of a little boy on Christmas morning. She smiled and opened the box. Her breath caught when she saw the diamond heart necklace sparkle against the dark background. "It's beautiful, but..."

"No buts, just promise me you'll wear it."

"Why, Dave? It's far too expensive a gift for..."

He took the box from her, removed the necklace, eased it around her neck and hooked it in back. "I like to see a beautiful woman wear diamonds, especially a woman who deserves them."

"Deserves them?" Before she could protest, his mouth covered hers and his arms drew her close. His hands roamed her back in small circles, every movement soothing and erotic. He deepened the kiss and tightened the embrace, and she knew she was lost. She could no longer deny she needed him, wanted him.

Ever so slowly, he ended the kiss. The look in his eyes said he understood her uncertainty but didn't share it.

He gently stroked her hair. "Do I scare you?"

"Scared isn't exactly what I'm feeling." She smiled, aware her voice was unsteady. She hadn't been this nervous since she wore her first strapless gown. He didn't frighten her, but what she was feeling toward him alarmed her. Love was a scary word, one she didn't dare utter.

"I'd never do anything to hurt you." He kissed her cheek, then the tip of her nose. "Do you believe me?"

"I don't know what I believe." She gently traced his hairline with the tips of her fingers. "If I'm afraid, it's because I question our judgment right now. Are we lovesick fools about to make the mistake of our lives?''

Dave laughed. ''I wouldn't call us fools.''

Her fingertips stilled over his lips. ''Is it possible then that our perspectives are clouded by hurt and anger?''

''It's possible, but it's also possible that I find you desirable, Jenny, and I hope you feel the same about me.'' His hand slipped to her shoulder and pushed fabric aside to reveal bare skin. ''If you're not ready for this, say the word and I'll stop.''

''Dave, I can't promise...''

''I'm not asking for promises. I want you, Jenny, because of who you are and how you make me feel.''

She closed her eyes to stop tears that threatened to start again. She wasn't sure what to make of his words, but she was sure of what she wanted from him.

He smoothed her hair from her face, then gently kissed her forehead. As she opened her mouth to speak she found his lips lowering to hers again. This time it was as if he was asking permission to love her, permission she granted with all her heart. She was tired of being alone, facing life by herself. He gave her a reason to go on, a will to succeed and overcome, a light in the face of darkness.

His lips tasted and invited as he stood up, pulling her with him. He lifted her into his arms and carried her up the long stairway. Propriety said stop, but her heart said hold on to him for as long as possible.

He kicked the door to his room open, carried her in and laid her on a soft mattress surrounded by an antique four-poster bed with a delicate lilac comforter and pillows.

He smiled apologetically. "This isn't my taste—it's my aunt's house."

"It's lovely."

"No, you're lovely."

With gentle finesse, he removed her T-shirt, then her bra. Her heart beat so fast she was afraid he'd hear it. As he lowered his head and his mouth closed over her breast, she had misgivings. She wanted him, every fiber in her body screamed for him, but was it right? Tomorrow, would she fervently wish she'd left before it was too late? She'd never been one for one-night stands. It was just emotions driving her, making her lose all control. They were both grieving for Dory. At this moment she needed what only he could give her.

Lowering his head, he deepened the kiss to a hungry urgency. The kiss wasn't the action of a man hellbent on having his way. It was the action of a man who wanted her, a saddened man who couldn't bear to spend another night alone. Her hands found the bottom of his Polo shirt, and she pulled it free from his pants, forcing him to stop his delicious assault while she eased the fabric over his head. Her hands roamed the bare expanse of his back and shoulders, and she felt his muscles tighten beneath her fingers.

He lifted his head to meet her eyes, silently questioning her, but she had no answers. Not tonight, certainly not in the morning.

"Are you sure?" He watched her nod. "One more kiss and you'll have no choice."

"I've made my choice," she whispered.

His hands slipped to her waist, unbuttoned her shorts, then inched them down her legs until they fell to the floor.

She shivered when his eyes devoured her. "Disappointed?"

"Not at all."

There was an unmistakable tingle in her abdomen as she reached for his belt. It wasn't the first time she'd been with a man, but her body was responding as if it was.

She heard a low groan deep in his throat as she freed him of his clothes. The desire in his eyes told her all she needed to know for now. He kissed her again, his fingers toying with the lace band of her panties, slipping under, then along the edge. He was torturing her with deliberate, masterful touches, his hand exploring every inch of the lacy fabric, inside and out.

Her breathing quickened as his tongue delved with an expertise far beyond her experience. Part of her wanted him to hurry, yet a deeper, darker part of her wanted the night to last forever. But bodies betrayed them. It had been too long, far too long.

A soft moan escaped her when he entered her. Time stopped, and he filled her, mind and body, his energy pouring into her, causing tremors of delight. The erotic scent of his skin filled her senses, the taste and feel of his kiss on her lips.

No foolish pride, no separate goals, only the need to erase the hurt.

Words were unnecessary. Bodies melded, satisfying each other to the limits of human endurance, seeking only the immediacy one could give to the other.

AFTERWARD, Jenny lay replete in the darkness, trying to make sense of their lovemaking. She had never been as uninhibited or as needy. What must he think of her?

Rolling to his side, Dave lifted a strand of her hair and kissed her neck. "Let's take a bubble bath."

"I don't know about that," she murmured. "You in bubbles?"

"Come on, it'll be fun. I haven't taken a bath with a beautiful woman in days."

"This should persuade me? You're crazy."

His eyes softened. "Crazy about you."

He scooped her up in his arms, carried her into the bathroom and playfully deposited her in the Jacuzzi. The warm water sloshed over her, and bubbles rose around her throat, lulling her into an erotic stupor.

Suddenly, candles along the rim of the tub flickered to life, their aromatic scent permeating the small room. He slid in beside her, and bubbles floated through the air. Her breath caught when his hands found her breasts, then smoothed over her stomach and below. When he pulled her to him, her legs circled his waist, and she clung to him, passion igniting. His lips were warm against hers, and in the small, steamy room, she floated to worlds she never knew existed.

"I want to make love to you again, only slower this time."

She moaned. "You must think—"

His mouth rested against hers. He whispered, "That you're terrific." His face sobered. "Stay here with me, Jenny."

She couldn't deny that she wanted to stay just as badly as he wanted her to.

Candlelight bathed the heated room. "And do what?" she parried.

"Oh, we'll think of something."

His mouth found hers, and she savored his tenderness, inhaling the fresh scent of bubbles and the feel of his arms around her. Of course, she would stay. How could she refuse?

Drops of water trickled from his hair and tickled her face. She pushed him away, laughing. "This is the first time I have ever seen your hair wet! You look so...cute."

Her giggle died to a smile. Was this really love she was feeling? Was it possible he was beginning to feel the same about her? She didn't dare ask, it was much too soon. They needed time to explore their new, erotic feelings. The last thing she wanted to do was scare him away. No, she'd take it slow and easy, one step at a time.

He tugged a lock of her wet hair. "Cute. You think I'm cute. What else do you think I am?"

She thought he was the most wonderful, caring man she had ever known. "Just cute, Kite Man. Don't push your luck."

"Kite Man, is it?" He pulled her into his arms and playfully dunked her under the water. When she emerged, spitting, he pinned her arms over her head and gave her a loud, smacking kiss.

"Ooh, that's bad—and not fair, either!"

His gaze adored her. "I'll show you fair."

She forgot fairness, and all else but the glorious sensations he caused inside her. Tomorrow was soon enough to think about her actions. For now, she wasn't going to think at all.

8

"STOP LOOKING AT ME." Princess got up and turned her backside to Jake.

He stared, head on paws, his eyes following the way her hips swayed as she strutted. "I'm still mad at you for landing me in the slammer."

"I had *nothing* to do with your incarceration." She sniffed and batted her eyes. "We have not talked since the incident. Was it horrible, monsieur?"

Jake snorted. "It weren't no picnic, honey."

"Did they...hurt you?"

"Naw, still just a little sore around the collar." Hell, he could stand anything they doled out—he'd only been in an hour.

She stared straight ahead. "Please, monsieur, stop looking at me."

Yawning and smacking his chops, he shifted positions. "I'm just thinking."

"About what?"

"Tryin' to figure out what goes through women's minds. You're either all over me or you won't let me look at you. What gives?"

She flipped her ears prettily, her tail wagging so fast it resembled a propeller. "Oh, you actually think? I thought all you did was dig."

There it is again. The bone. Why doesn't she come right out and say it? Confront me! Hell, honey, confrontation is my middle name. Come on. Fight. Show me your stuff.

She stuck her nose in the air, ignoring his aggressive glare.

"Don't act so hoity-toity, sister. You may as well get used to me being around."

"I beg your pardon?"

"You heard me, Frenchie. My human and your human are gettin' pretty cozy. I tell ya, the way they looked at each other this morning, I got the impression that you and I may be eating out of the same dish soon."

She tossed her head. "Never!"

Twist that little fanny all you want, sugar. Mark my words—we're gonna be roomies.

"Believe me, monsieur, my human is much too busy to have time for such nonsense."

"Nonsense?"

"You know—romance."

Jake rose, walked over and sniffed her. "Listen, Frenchie, where I come from, if you're too busy for romance, cover yourself with dirt, 'cause you're dead."

Princess swatted him with her paw. "I would expect such foolishness from a lowly bouledogue." She daintily settled herself on her cushion. "Personally, I don't think our humans even like each other. They're always spatting over the baby."

Jake laid down opposite her. "Yeah, but the baby's

gone now, heh, heh, heh." He wiggled his brows sug-
gestively. "Or as you say in France, ooh, la, la."

"Ooh, la, garbage." She jumped up and pounced
on him, then walked to the end of her chain. "Take
your dirty mind to your side of the tree."

Jake raised himself to a sitting position when he
heard the kite shop door open. He settled down, head
on paws.

*Like I said, sugar, as sure as there's fleas, we're
gone be roomies.*

LEANING CLOSER to the mirror, Jenny rubbed the dark
circles under her eyes. For a smart woman, she was
acting like an imbecile. Mooning over a man with
whom she should only be friends. She couldn't believe she'd fallen into bed with Dave Kasada. Did he
think she was easy? Apparently. Every time she
started to bring up that night, he changed the subject.
He came around the store less now that Dory was
gone, but she figured he was busy organizing his
move. It was hard to put their relationship in perspective. She'd discovered the cliché that the earth
moved was true, but Dave refused to discuss it. She
couldn't understand her behavior. She didn't go to
bed with every man she met. Why Dave?

Why now?

She groaned.

Why me?

The telephone rang as she walked into the kitchen.
"Hello?"

"Hi, it's Mark."

"Hi, Mark. Everything okay with the financial report?" She'd finally faxed it late yesterday afternoon.

"It's a go. The committee met this morning, and you're approved for the loan."

Jenny sank against the counter. She'd been hoping, but nothing had gone the way she'd planned lately.

"Sign the papers and the money is yours."

"Fantastic. I'll have Mrs. Wilcox come in early Thursday so I can get away." She hung up, relieved. Now all she had to do was contract the carpenters, knock out a wall and order the new counters.

A clap of thunder shook the house as she buttered a bagel and poured coffee into an insulated cup. Rain. All she needed. Lathering blackberry jam on the bagel, she wondered why Dave hadn't mentioned the date he'd be moving. Soon, she hoped, but she would miss not having him next door. She missed him not popping in to play with Dory.

Picking up a rattle of Dory's that had been left behind, she bit her lower lip. She hadn't heard a word from Rob and Teensy. Had they arrived in New York safely? It had been over three weeks. You would think they could drop a note and let her know everything was okay. Labor Day was right around the corner, and she still didn't have permanent help. Mrs. Wilcox was complaining she'd gained ten pounds and desperately needed to find another line of work.

"Come on, Princess, we're running late." Jenny stuck the bagel in her mouth and scooped the dog up with her other arm. "Gee, girl. You putting on weight?"

MRS. WILCOX was just hanging up the phone when Jenny walked into the shop. She shook out her raincoat and hung it up to dry.

"There you are."

"Hi, been busy?"

Mrs. Wilcox ripped a page off the order pad and handed it to Jenny as she breezed past on her way to the back room. "Not bad yet. I think the rain has kept it down. Oh, a large phone order just came in."

"Oh?" Jenny's muffled voice came from the storeroom.

"The White House, no less. They want twenty-two dozen fudgeballs for a formal dinner at the end of the week." Mrs. Wilcox wasn't able to hide the excitement in her voice as she smoothed her burgeoning hips. "God have mercy."

"Twenty-two dozen?"

"Some ambassador's comin' to town. Didn't say who. A congressman named Nelson visited the island in June and fell in love with the candy. The White House wanted to know if we could fill the order on short notice, and I said yes. Hope you don't mind, but I knew you wouldn't want to lose the business."

"I can't afford to lose it." Jenny dropped a sack of sugar on the counter.

"I told them twenty-two dozen wouldn't be a problem. They want the candy tied in red, white and blue ribbons. We're instructed to overnight them."

"We'll get right to work on it."

Jenny's stomach rolled as she dumped sugar, corn syrup and cream into the copper vat. For a moment she felt light-headed. Moreover, the sight of the gooey mixture turned her stomach. Maybe she'd made one too many fudgeballs, or she was coming down with a bug. Her breath caught, and she suddenly felt faint. She frantically counted the days since her last period. Thirty-six—it couldn't be. She was still on the pill. There was no way she could… Impossible! One night, that was all!

Dave came into the store, empty coffee cup in hand. "I'm out of coffee again. I hope you have some."

Jenny nodded toward the back room, avoiding eye contact. He'd been so scarce lately she was surprised to see him. Fate?

One crummy night! She couldn't be pregnant. It was much too soon to suffer morning sickness. Her mind rebelled. She couldn't be. It was that two o'clock refrigerator raid this morning—cold lasagna—

Dave emerged from the back room stirring powdered creamer into his coffee. He came up behind her and he watched over her shoulder as she stirred candy. The scent of his after-shave heightened her queasiness. "You haven't said anything about the movers—you want me to call them?"

She glanced up. "You haven't *done* that?" He took a sip of coffee, his eyes grazing her lightly. She felt warm, then hot under his close scrutiny.

"No— I thought you'd take care of it."

Geez, her expression said.

Damn, his implied.

He shrugged. "Well, one of us needs to do it. What's good? The first of the month?"

"Or sooner," she agreed. The first was a week away. The sooner he was out, the sooner she could get the carpenters in there. She dumped a pound of butter into the vat. Should she tell him she was taking over his space or just do it and then tell him? He would be so busy with the move he wouldn't notice for awhile, then she would break it to him gently. Not that he'd care, but barging in on his former space seemed insensitive, as if she'd planned it—which she *had,* but she didn't want him to know. Mackinac City wasn't the end of the earth. Just because he wouldn't be next door didn't mean they wouldn't bump into each other. She fought the sudden urge to cry, knowing it wasn't going to be the same without him next door.

She made a conscious effort to steer her thoughts in another direction. "Heard any more from Megan?"

"Not a thing." His response was curt and to the point. She got the hint.

Lifting a large tray, she said softly, "Well, the waiting's almost over. Labor Day's right around the corner."

It was after lunch before she got around to calling the carpenters. When they asked for measurements, she realized she didn't have any. How was she going to measure without alerting Dave to her plans? What possible excuse could she use to measure his walls? Promising to call right back, she located a tape measure and ducked next door. Dave was on the phone when she walked in the kite shop. She glanced around the store, dismayed to see he hadn't packed a single box yet.

She waved to him, silently mouthing, "Got a pair of scissors?" A pretty lame excuse, but it should suffice.

He nodded, going on with his conversation as he reached into the drawer for the scissors.

While he was distracted, she measured from front to back, then sideways. Starting at the back of the counter, she carefully stepped off the feet, allowing for at least eight additional feet up front, near the large plate glass window. Customers liked to watch the candy being made, plus the chocolaty smells drew them to the shop like a magnet. The new counters would be near the back, so that would mean she'd need to knock out the east wall—maybe even two walls.

She snapped the tape closed and wrote down the figures.

Dave looked up, frowning.

She lifted her brows, grinning. "Got any glue?"

He rummaged around in the drawer as he automatically answered the person on the other end of the line.

She stepped to the far wall and studied it. The walls were painted white. A nice paisley paper would brighten up the space, or maybe one of those large floral prints that were so popular. Spreading both arms flat against the surface, she inched her way slowly down the length of the wall. It was a lot bigger than it looked. It would take ten to twelve double rolls, maybe thirteen.

She paused and wrote it down, then glanced up to see Dave staring at her.

Covering the receiver with his hand, he asked, "Is there something I can help you with?"

"No, don't let me bother you. I'll only be a minute. Do you know how many gallons of paint it took to paint the back wall?"

His frown deepened. "Aren't the walls in your shop the same size?"

"No." She studied the partition. "I think these might be a little bigger."

His eyes measured the area. "I don't know—couple gallons, I guess."

"Thanks." She wrote it down.

"Something wrong with the walls on your side? Do they need painting?"

"No, they're in pretty good shape."

Scissors and glue in hand, she went out the door, still figuring on the notepad.

WHEN SHE GOT HOME that night, she threw open the front door of her cottage, headed straight to the bathroom and threw up. Fumbling for a wet cloth, she leaned weakly on the side of the stool, praying. "Please, please, please, let it be bad lasagna."

She closed her eyes and tried to imagine telling Dave he was about to be a father again. Oh, he'd *want* the child. She didn't doubt that. But what about her? Would he want *her?* She was past telling herself she hadn't fallen in love with him. *That night* burned in her mind like an acetylene torch, forcing her to admit she wanted more out of life than a display case full of fudgeballs.

She hurled the cloth across the room. It was so

unfair! She hadn't been irresponsible. She'd been on the pill for years. Had the pill failed? Leaning back, she closed her eyes as horror stories of women getting pregnant while on the pill flooded her mind. All those years with Brian... Her eyes widened. Thank God it wasn't Brian's baby.

Those tests. She had to buy one of those home pregnancy tests. But everyone on the island would know what she was doing if she marched into the pharmacy and bought one.

She stood, stepped to the sink, splashed water on her face and headed to the kitchen, where she made a cup of tea to calm herself. She had to think rationally. Give it another day or two. She'd had late periods before—not often, but once or twice in her teens. Five days late once, and she'd been a virgin. There was absolutely nothing to be concerned about. It was a false alarm. With the expansion plans and the extra work at the store, it was a stress reaction.

Relax, she told herself. *Tomorrow you'll laugh about it.*

THE TEENAGE CLERK glanced up as Jenny took her purchase to the counter. She'd been lurking between the pharmacy and cosmetic aisles for over thirty minutes. When the last customer left the store, she hurried to the counter with her easy one-step pregnancy test. She set the test down, then stacked an *Enquirer* and a couple of packs of gum on top of it. She mentally groaned when she saw that the clerk was the daughter of a friend, but she couldn't wait another minute. She had to know.

"Hi, ya, Miss McNeill." The girl shoved the magazine and gum aside, then picked up the test box and read it.

Jenny felt heat creeping up her neck and was sure she was turning a bright shade of red. "The, uh, price is on—"

"Mrs. Luttrell!" the teenager called out. "How much is the One Step Clear Blue home pregnancy test? It's not marked!"

"It's not?"

"No!"

"I'll look!"

Jenny prayed for a tidal wave to swamp the island.

"On special. Sixteen ninety-eight."

"Thanks!" The clerk turned to Jenny. "On special. It's your lucky day."

Oh, yes, real lucky. She had all those fudgeballs to make and package, and she was sick as a dog and humiliated to the core.

The girl rang up the test, the magazine and the gum. "Anything else?"

"No, thank you." She paid, then got out of there.

Pedaling home, she wondered how long it would take for the news to spread. Two hours, max, she was betting.

"You bought a pregnancy test?"

Jenny checked her watch. Forty-three and a half minutes. The gossips were upping productivity. Leaning against the door frame, she crossed her arms. "Don't you think that's a little personal?"

Dave sobered. "I think if you're pregnant, it involves me."

Their gazes locked.

"You don't know that."

"I'd bet the new kite line on it."

"Are you implying that I'm trying to trap you into marriage?"

Irritation tinged his face. "Come on, Jenny. This is the nineties. Trap me?"

"Well, don't worry, I'm not going to corner you. I'm a few days late. I think it's stress, but I want to be sure."

"Look, Jenny—"

She pushed away from the door. "No, *you* look. If there's anything to tell, I'll let you know." She shut the door and leaned against it for support. How dare he confront her about something so personal? How dare he assume that he— That she— How *dare* he! Who'd told *him*, of all people that she'd bought a pregnancy kit?

Had his first reaction been anger or concern?

Sinking to the floor, she buried her face in her hands. How had her life become so darn complicated?

PACING IN THE BATHROOM, Jenny checked her watch for the fourth time. Thirty seconds had passed since the last time she checked. Impatient, she grabbed the box that had held the pregnancy test and reread the instructions.

"Easy one step. Use any time of day. Over ninety-nine percent accurate. Results in three minutes." She looked at her watch again, tapped it, put it to her ear, heard nothing and sat on the toilet seat, exasperated. Of course, she would hear nothing—it was battery operated. She tossed the empty box in the trash and checked the time again. "Two minutes. One to go."

She felt foolish talking to herself, but it was either that or go nuts. Too late. She was already nuts, certifiably crazy. Crazy for her life to hinge on a slender stick, crazy for straining to see one line for negative or two for positive.

"One, two, buckle my shoe—come on, come on. Bingo!"

One line. Her eyes strained to make sure. Definitely only one line.

Running from the confined quarters to the living room, she shouted, "Hallelujah!"

She dropped to the sofa and drew her knees up. Negative. Sudden tears pricked her eyes. She swiped at them, confused. Surely she didn't want to be pregnant, did she? Or did she? She stretched out flat on her back and ran her hands over her smooth stomach. Sadness engulfed her.

Dave would be relieved. At least he'd know she wasn't trying to trap him into marriage. He hadn't actually said that, but he'd had a look on his face like a deer caught in headlights. She rubbed her stomach again. Why wasn't she happy? She turned on her side and curled up in a fetal position.

Hating herself for thinking it, she pictured herself married to Dave, babies and puppies running through the house. Crazy. She was really bonkers. She was even starting to like Jake, darn it.

She rolled off the sofa, walked into the kitchen,

picked up the phone and dialed. "Dave? It's me. I just wanted you to know …it's a false alarm.…Yes, positive—no, no, the test is negative. I'm positive the test is negative.…Well, it would have complicated things." Was that wistfulness she heard in his voice, echoed in hers? It couldn't be. She wasn't emotionally ready for all that a pregnancy would entail. Even if Dave agreed that matrimony would be the proper course, she wouldn't marry him. Would she?

Reluctantly she dressed for work, feeling empty and alone for the first time in her life. Even the expansion and her booming business lacked luster today, but she had to move forward. There were all those fudgeballs that had to reach the White House tomorrow by air express. At best, she would be working late into the night.

She worked fast and furiously the rest of the day, but it was still an hour past closing time before the Closed sign was pulled into place, and she still had three more batches of fudgeballs to cool and wrap.

"I'd be glad to stay," Mrs. Wilcox offered, "but the mister gets testy when I'm not there to fix his supper. I could come back.…"

"No, I'll finish up. Here." She handed the older lady a box of misshapen fudgeballs. "Take these to Mr. Wilcox."

"Oh, he'll love it!" The woman beamed and sampled a couple.

"Have a nice evening, Mrs. Wilcox. I'll see you in the morning."

Jenny locked the door, then turned to look at the copper kettle. She was beginning to hate that thing.

Hours later, her aching back told her it was late—later than she realized. She moaned when she glanced at the clock and saw it was two in the morning. Leaving the last batch to cool, she walked to the front window and glanced out. The full moon bathed the deserted streets in mellow light. She rubbed her tight shoulders. A Kasada backrub would feel good about now. A Kasada anything would feel good.

Light filtered from the kite shop onto the front walk, and she wondered what was going on. Of course, he was packing. She stepped out the door, leaving it ajar for fresh air. She smiled at the poodle sleeping soundly on her cushion. She was reluctant to leave her out so late, but Princess couldn't stay in the store.

She cupped her hands to her eyes and peeked into the kite shop window. Dave was behind the counter, bent over his workbench, Jake at his feet.

When she opened the door and stepped inside, Jake flew past her. "I'm sorry. Jake?"

"He won't go anywhere, and I hope Dogcatcher Harris is sleeping right now."

She laughed and walked closer. "You have a big order for the White House, too?"

He chuckled softly. "I haven't heard from Clinton in—oh, days. Obviously, he doesn't like kites as well as he likes fudge."

Leaning on the counter, she propped her chin on her hands and stared at him. There wasn't a sign of a packed box or crate around. Men. "What are you doing here so late?"

He kept his eyes on the kite he was stringing. "Couldn't sleep. I'm worried about Megan."

His eyes looked more than tired. They looked incredibly sad. Was he worried about more than his daughter? "Dave, I should have stopped by earlier. You must have been concerned when you heard about the pregnancy test."

"Oh, that. No, I wasn't concerned. Just surprised."

Yes, he *was* surprised, she remembered. "Well, you can rest. I told you over the phone, I'm not pregnant."

His gaze rose to meet hers, his brows knitted.

Her laugh came out a nervous twitter. "You act as if you're disappointed. I thought you'd be happy— ecstatically so."

Turning to his kite, he shook his head, "Don't be silly. Of course, I'm happy. Aren't you happy?"

"Sure, same as you. A baby would complicate my life right now."

"Yeah, they can do that."

She averted her head as tears sprang to her eyes. What was wrong with her? Twice today, she'd had to stop and have a good cry. She should be immensely relieved. Instead she felt disappointed and empty. This morning her period had started. Had she waited another day, she wouldn't have had to take the pregnancy test. All it did was spread gossip about her around town and alarm Dave unnecessarily.

She sniffed into a tissue. "I have to go—have to finish up the White House order." As she turned to leave, he reached out and took her by the shoulder.

"Is something wrong?"

"Wrong? No, what could be wrong?" She sniffed again, and he turned her to face him. His features softened, and his gaze caressed her. She wanted to dissolve into his arms and sob her heart out. "I—I'm sorry—I've been an emotional wreck all day."

He tipped her chin with the crook of his finger. "Anything I can do to help?"

She shook her head. "No. I don't have anything to cry about. I guess I'm just tired."

He stepped away, and she felt suddenly abandoned. "You work too hard."

"Is there any other way to work?"

He laughed and picked up the kite he was working on. "What do you think? It's my new design."

She studied it, blew her nose, then said, "It's great. What are you calling it?"

"Sky Walker."

She nodded, then hung her head. "Oh, Dave, I'm sorry. Lately, I've been so...so— I can't even explain."

He put the kite down and returned to her side, draping his arm around her shoulder. "You know what? I think we miss Dory. I know I do."

She leaned into him. He smelled like Irish Spring soap. "I can still hear her squeals when she would see me in the morning—"

"And that silly little giggle when I'd tickle her belly."

Just thinking about it made Jenny smile. "I hope she's all right. I thought Rob would write." Her merriment trickled to a smile, then sadness overtook her. Her hand slid to her stomach. No baby. "I have to get back to work.'' She pulled away and walked toward the door.

"Yeah, I think I'll call it a night—or morning, or whatever."

He disappeared into the back room, and she let herself out. Thirty more minutes and she could drop into bed, exhausted.

She let out a scream as she walked into the store and saw Jake and Princess standing in the middle of the table of cooling fudgeballs, knocking them on to the floor, clearly in the midst of a fun new game. Her gaze flew to a nearby chair that was tipped over. Likely they'd used it to reach the table.

Furious, she grabbed Princess and without thinking paddled her behind. "You have never misbehaved in your life! What's gotten into you?" Whirling on Jake, she yelled, "You! Get off this table!" She smacked him with a flyswatter. "You're teaching Princess bad habits—you've ruined the President's balls!"

She couldn't believe she said that.

"Fudgeballs!" she amended, screeching.

The dogs flew to the back room, yelping.

She could hear Dave whistling for his dog. "Here, Jake." Whistle, whistle. "Where are you, boy?"

Boy? She fumed. *Boy* had just demolished the White House fudge! It would take another six hours to cook, cool and pack twenty-six dozen.

The door of the fudge shop opened, and Dave stuck his head in. "Jenny, have you seen—"

Jake came boiling out of the back, Princess on his heels. Both dogs were yapping at the top of their lungs.

"Jake!" he bellowed, holding Princess's broken collar in his hand. "I had a feeling he might be here when I found this." He held out what was left of the pink rhinestone-studded collar.

"Too bad he didn't run to China!" she shouted, making no attempt to cover her disgust.

His gaze took in the carnage, and he frowned. "What happened?"

Too furious to speak, she could only point at the table of smashed, half-eaten fudgeballs. Finding her voice, she spoke through gritted teeth. "Get your *dog* out of my sight before I string him up by his hind legs! He's ruined my candy and involved Princess in his recklessness."

Dave stiffened. "Now wait a minute. Princess was in on this, too, wasn't she?"

"Jake was the ringleader!" Jenny shrieked. "That's a White House order! He's just ruined a huge account! I'll have to stay up the rest of the night to make new ones. The fudgeballs have to be on the morning flight to Washington!"

"It's not the end of the world." Dave studied the gooey carnage. "Call Bill and tell him two dogs ate his fudge—" His hand shot up. "*Don't* throw that spoon at me." Frowning, he reached for an apron. "Just tell me what to do and I'll help."

"I'm in no mood for corny jokes. Go home." She snatched an apron off a peg and wrapped it around her waist. "When are you moving?" she grumbled. She was tired, out of sorts and weepy. An already rotten day had just been topped off with this. "I've had it with your dog—"

"What?"

She refused to look at him. "I said when are you moving?"

"Wait a minute." He put a spoon down. "What do you mean, when am *I* moving? You've got it backward, haven't you? I'm not moving—you're moving, to Mackinac City."

She whirled. "No, *you're* moving to Mackinac City. I'm moving into your space." There. She'd said it, and he knew. It was out, and she was relieved.

He advanced on her, his eyes narrowed. "Let me get this straight. You think you're moving into my space—the kite shop?"

She lifted her chin. "Yes."

"Are you *nuts?* What about Loyal? The lease?"

"What about Loyal and the lease? That's *your* problem. I've *made* all the arrangements for you."

"You *what?*"

Was he hard of hearing? "I looked at the new space with you. You wanted my approval, I gave it. You were too busy to call Loyal and asked me to do it. I called Loyal, and he wanted to know about the lease, I told you, you said you'd call him—"

"I *did* call him—to set up your lease! I even sent him the damn money as a favor to you. I thought you were having financial troubles!"

"*Me?* I'm not having financial troubles—or I wasn't until now!" The implication of his words was beginning to sink in. There had been a colossal misunderstanding. Sickness washed over her. She wasn't going to move her store. She didn't have the money to move. "My loan is only for the expansion in the building I occupy. It's not enough to cover the Mackinac City property."

"Where in the hell did you ever get the idea you could take over my floor space?"

She stiffened. "Hank Linstrom told me I could have it, that you didn't have a lease."

He held his hand up to stop her. "Hank Linstrom is no longer employed by Rockfield."

She lifted her chin. "How do *you* know so much about Mr. Linstrom?"

"*I'm* the one who fired him, damn it."

"You?" This was nuts! She hated arguments—especially when she didn't know what the hell they were talking about.

He crossed his arms arrogantly. "I own Rockfield."

It took a moment for the information to soak in. When it did, she knew her moving into the kite shop space was a moot point. She felt confused, stunned, disappointed, but mostly angry and hurt. "Why didn't Mr. Linstrom tell me you owned... More importantly, why didn't *you* tell me?"

"It never came up." He ran his fingers through his hair. "I know you're upset, I should have told you, but when you started making arrangements to move out—or at least I thought you were—I didn't see the need."

"Didn't see the *need?*" Her anger rocketed.

"Look, Jenny, I know you're hurt. This is all a crazy misunderstanding, but we can work it out. I can loan you the money to move to Mackinac City—"

"You know what you can do with your money,

Dave Kasada. I don't want your money, your excuses, your dog, and most of all, I don't want you! Now get out!'' She shoved him toward the door.

"Dammit, be reasonable! We're adults, we can work this—''

"Forget it.'' She'd had enough for one day. She'd had enough for a lifetime!

She slammed the door shut, then immediately opened it again.

"And that goes for your dog, too!''

9

JAKE HUDDLED DEEPER into the folds of his skin. "If it wasn't for your sweet tooth, we wouldn't be in this trouble. I get blamed for everything."

"I don't understand," Princess fretted. "I just can't get enough candy lately. I never liked it before. And you know what else?"

Jake yawned and smacked his lips. "There's more?"

"I have this craving for a big...T-bone."

The bone. She's not getting the bone. She can wag that tail as fast as she wants. She's not getting the bone. "Yeah? You look different. You puttin' on weight?"

Princess burst into tears, whining, "Just a few weeks ago, you told me I had the best figure on a poodle you'd ever seen."

"I'm not sayin' you're fat," he growled. "I just thought you'd filled out some. I ain't sayin' it don't look good on you—"

She whined louder.

"Oh, cripes," Jake huffed, "I can't say anything lately without you bawling. What's wrong now?"

Princess wiped her eye dry with her paw. "I don't

know. My human gets something called PMS. Do you think I might have caught it?''

Jake raised his head and studied her. "PMS? Yeah, that's it. Poodle Misery Syndrome. You must have a touch of it.''

Whimpering, she laid her head on his neck. "I'm feeling so blue. I miss having a baby around.''

Jake scooted close to her and let out a quivering breath. "Me, too.''

THE NEXT MORNING, Jenny stirred nuts into a nearly cooled vat of fudge, trying to vent her anger. She wasn't sure who she'd like to shoot first—Loyal the Realtor for not being specific, Dave for not telling her who he really was or the dogs for destroying the White House fudge.

Lack of sleep was getting to her. She reached to rub her shoulder and her hand caught in the chain around her neck. The thin gold strained, then she felt it slip. Her eye caught the twinkle of a diamond as it fell into the vat of fudge. "No!" she yelled, trying to catch it before it sank to the bottom.

"Something wrong, dearie?''

"Everything is wrong, Mrs. Wilcox.'' She stuck her arm deep into the sticky, warm chocolate, her fingers desperately searching for the diamond heart.

Mrs. Wilcox watched her dig around in the vat of fudge. "You feelin' all right?''

"Fine, thanks.'' She felt like crap. She had a loan for expansion and nowhere to go. Dave, the kindly kite master, had turned into Attila the Hun, avoiding her like the flu. Her feet hurt, and the new antibacterial soap had caused an ugly rash to break out on her hands.

Where was her necklace? She wedged her other arm in and began to dig through the cooling fudge. She should leave it in the middle of a fudgeball and feed it to Kite Man. No. No matter how mad she was right now, his gift meant a lot to her, and she had to find it. Thick chocolate covered her arms up to her elbows. If that wasn't bad enough, the entire batch would have to be made over. Again.

"New method of making fudge?"

Jenny lifted her head to see Dave standing in the doorway. "It's the personal touch."

He smiled. "At least you're talking to me."

She groaned and pulled her arms out of the vat. "Not really. We have nothing to say to each other." It still unnerved her to learn the man she'd fallen in love with was a consummate liar. How could he have tricked her about who he was?

"Jenny, be reasonable about this." He followed her into the back room where she washed her arms in the mop sink. "Can't we at least discuss it?"

"Why? So you can say, 'Jenny, I forgot to mention I own this building and plan to throw you out on your fanny because I want to expand the kite shop?'" She turned and walked to the front with him close on her heels.

"Wasn't that what you were about to do to me?"

She turned to look at him. "No. I was helping you find a place."

"No." He crossed his arms. "*I* was helping *you* relocate. I thought it was all settled. *I* called Loyal, made arrangements for us to see the property, you liked it, said it looked great to you, so *I* called Loyal back and told him to draw up a lease, at your instruction.''

''My instruction? *I* told Loyal to draw up the lease at *your* instruction.''

''I sent a deposit!''

''That's because you're the one moving, not me!''

''Children.'' Mrs. Wilcox came out of the back room. ''Customers will hear you.''

Jenny glanced to see a few people standing near the counter. Lowering her voice, she issued a curt, formal request. ''Will you kindly step into the storeroom.''

He followed her to the back, pinching off a piece of fudge as he passed the marble cooling table.

''Don't do that.''

Her anger threatened to recede as she perused his khaki slacks and blue Polo shirt. Why did he always have to look so darn good? She hadn't realized how much she needed him—yes, she needed him. Not just physically, but emotionally. Who was she kidding? All she could think about lately was him and how she wished she *had* been carrying his child. If Fudgeballs had to leave the Island, she'd never see him again.

When they entered the dark storage room, she opened her mouth to say something then closed it when he drew her into his arms and kissed her. It felt so good to be in his arms. He made her feel safe and protected. Through all the misunderstandings, her feelings hadn't changed. The taste of his lips and the musky scent of his skin still affected her in a magical way. She wished they were alone, where the feel of his naked body against hers would momentarily assuage their problems.

When their lips parted, he wouldn't let her go. "Will you listen to me? I'm sorry I didn't tell you I own Rockfield, but it didn't seem important at the time. Hell, it *wasn't* important until a few weeks ago."

She met his steady gaze. "You lied to me."

"When? I have never once lied to you."

"You misled me, then. Why didn't you tell me I was the one moving instead of letting me think you were about to vacate your space?"

"It was a hell of a misunderstanding, but you can't blame me. You should have told me what you were planning to do."

Her courage wilted along with her anger. Slumping against his chest, she let him hold her. "What am I going to do? I can't afford to rent the space in Mackinac City—not yet. All my money has to go toward the expansion—new equipment. It's the only way the bank will fund me."

"If it's just money you're worried about, don't be. I can loan—"

Pulling away, she wiped her nose. "I wouldn't hear of it."

He took her arm. "Jenny, don't be a fool. Fudgeballs is growing. You've got a good thing going. Don't let pride make you throw it away."

"I can't borrow another cent, Dave. I'm already in hock up to my eyeballs. The expansion would have doubled my profit, but now that can't happen. I'll have to struggle along in the space I have.'' Her hand felt for the necklace that was no longer there. Tears burned her lids. ''And there's something else you need to know.''

''You're going to buy Rockfield Corporation so you can stay here and throw me out?''

''Be serious.'' Her fingers clutched at her throat. ''I lost the necklace in a batch of fudge.''

He wiped a tear from her cheek. ''I'll buy you another one.''

''I want *that* one.''

''Why do you insist on being difficult?''

''I'm sorry, Dave. I—''

''Dearie,'' Mrs. Wilcox yelled through the open doorway. ''Making fudge balls really paid off today. Look!'' She held up a brown blob. ''There're diamonds in the candy!'' She handed Jenny the necklace.

Jenny's heart skipped a beat when she saw the heart embedded in the fudge. ''Thank you.''

''Oh, Mr. Kasada, Mrs. Kasada is on the phone.''

Dave swore under his breath, releasing Jenny's arm. ''Hold off making any decisions for a few days. Let me see what I can do. I'll talk to you later tonight.''

He left, and all she could do was stare at the door. Exactly what did he think he could do? she thought resentfully.

She was the one out in the cold.

DAVE PICKED UP the phone.

''I'm back, and we need to talk,'' Nancy said curtly.

No Hello, how are you, sorry I haven't written to let you know how Megan is doing. Just, We need to talk. Well, she was right about that. They did need to talk. "Where's Megan?"

"She's here, and she's fine. Sorry I haven't gotten back with you," Nancy apologized. "What's your schedule like?"

"I'm not too busy to have my daughter, if that's what you mean."

"Can you get away for a few days, come to Chicago? We honestly need to talk, Dave, and not over the phone."

"What's this about, Nancy?" He knew her tricks, and he wasn't falling for them.

"Megan."

The solemnity of her voice scared him. What did she have up her sleeve this time? Full custody of Megan? Of course. She and her rich husband wanted it all, money, power *and* his daughter.

"Forget it, Nancy."

"Dave, control your temper. This is serious. We need to talk. Can you be in Chicago by the end of the week?"

Dave snapped a pencil in half.

"Dave?"

"I can be there by Friday."

"Good. I'll have Father draw up papers—"

"The hell you will! You won't do anything until I get there!" He held the receiver away from his ear as she hung up on him.

Have *Father* draw up papers? The salt air must have corroded her brain. She'd be in for the fight of her life if she thought he would relinquish custody of Megan. Jonathan Pharis might be loaded, but he didn't have a crutch to stand on when it came down to it. Dave was a good father, and no one and no amount of money could change that.

JENNY WAS ROUSED from a deep sleep by the doorbell. Rolling over to look at the clock, she groaned. Two o'clock. What nut was ringing her doorbell at this hour?

Scratching her head, she padded to the door, trying to focus. The two aspirin she'd taken earlier had her head spinning like a top.

She leaned against the doorway, closing her eyes. "Who is it?"

"Dave. Can I come in?"

"You selling cookies or something?"

"Let me in, Jenny."

She yawned, unlatched the door and let it swing open. She stepped back as a rush of cool air trickled through her thin nightie.

Dave brushed past her. "Did I wake you?"

She closed the door, wondering why she hadn't grabbed a robe. "Of course, you woke me." Pushing away from the door frame, she went into the kitchen. He followed.

"What are you doing up this time of the night?"

"I couldn't sleep."

She filled the coffeepot with water. "Trouble?"

"Nancy wants me in Chicago by Friday."

"Oh?" She measured coffee into a filter. She'd

wondered all day about the significance of the call. "Did she say why?"

"Something to do with Megan. I think she's going to ask me to let Pharis adopt her." He took a seat at the kitchen table. "I'll never allow that, Jenny. I can't."

Jenny sat across from him. "I know."

"I *won't* sign away my daughter. Nancy can be cruel, but even as coldhearted as she is, taking Megan is..."

"Dave, calm down," Jenny said, laying her hand over his on the table. "You don't know that's what she wants. Just wait and see. You could be wrong."

"I have a one hell of a headache." He rubbed his temples to ease the dull throb. "Do you have any aspirin?"

"I'll get it, and the coffee."

HE WATCHED HER leave the room, the sight of her oddly comforting. He needed her tonight like he'd never needed anyone before. She was his sanity. She was the only person who understood what he was going through, and he thanked God he had her.

It wouldn't surprise him if Nancy had found out he'd been seeing Jenny and wanted to punish him by taking Megan. Possible, but not probable. None of Nancy's friends hung around the island—it wasn't posh enough, and it certainly wasn't the south of France.

"Here you go," Jenny said, setting the aspirin in front of him.

He stared at the bottle, the words on the label blurring in front of his eyes. Jenny pulled him from his morbid thoughts when she set a glass of water and a cup of coffee in front of him. "Thanks," he muttered, tossing two tablets into his mouth.

She listened quietly as he complained about life in general, his gaze slipping to the gap in the front of her thin robe and the outline of her nipples that showed through the filmy fabric.

"Dave?" Jenny shook her head. "You haven't heard a word I've said."

"You said you wanted to tuck me in your bed and make me feel better, didn't you?" He smiled when she blushed and averted her gaze.

"You're pretty frisky for a man with a headache."

She met his gaze across the table, and her eyes told him she wasn't adverse to the idea. Reaching for his hand, she stood and walked toward the living room. "I never should have given you that coffee. You're much too awake for this time of the morning."

He followed her down the hall of her quaint little cottage into the bedroom on the right. "Pink?" he asked, eyeing the very feminine decor.

"I'm a woman. We like pink." She sat on the bed and patted the mattress beside her. "Come on, pink won't kill you."

"You sure?" He sat, stretching tired muscles.

"Your aunt Mosie's lavender didn't, did it?" Her hands slipped to his shoulders. "Let me work the kinks out of your neck." Eventually, she helped him pull off the green knit Polo and made him lie on his stomach.

"You're getting a little bossy." He didn't have the

strength to argue with her. Her soft hands felt like heaven, and the tenseness in his shoulders began to melt as she worked her magic.

Her hands kneaded sore muscles and worked on knots of stress that had formed since the phone call. He felt the softness of her lips touch the center of his back. Her tongue teased a trail to his belt line then up again. Did she know what she was doing to him? He groaned and tried to roll over.

"I'm not done with you yet," she said.

"I certainly hope not."

She kissed him lightly on the lips. "Talk about bossy…"

He rolled to his back and loosened the sash around her waist, then pushed the robe from her shoulders. The short opaque gown left little to the imagination, stirring the heat that already throbbed in his groin.

"Miss McNeill, what will people say?"

"Are you complaining, Mr. Kasada?"

"Hardly." He opened his mouth as she lowered her lips to his. The sweet scent of her perfume was like an erotic elixir that seeped into his every pore. Her fingers threaded through the mat of hair on his chest, her kiss sheer pleasure.

She filled the void in his heart with feelings he never thought he'd have. It was love she gave, and he selfishly took all she offered. He wanted her, not just for the night, but to be his partner. A woman like her came along only once, and he was determined not to lose her.

His hands found the bottom of her gown and slipped inside, closing over her breasts. As she ended the kiss and sat up, he pulled the thin garment off her and feasted on her natural beauty. ''What would I do without you?''

Her eyes softened in the light of the full moon that streamed through the open window, casting shadows over her nakedness. She was a sight to behold, and he memorized her every curve with his hands.

She pushed away without a word and knelt to pull off his shoes and socks, then his belt. He watched the spark of desire grow in her hazel eyes. He took a deep breath and held it while she licked her lips and smiled. She made quick work of his clothes then lay beside him.

Moonlight kissed her tan body as he rolled over and kissed her throat, working his way over her breasts to her stomach. The salty taste of her skin mixed with the scent of bath soap as he worked his way up to her lips.

There were no words to describe his need for her. His love went far beyond simple physical pleasure. She'd become a part of him, consuming his every thought, day and night. He wanted her with him always.

She moaned sweetly when he entered her warmth, and she wrapped her legs possessively around him. He wanted to tell her how precious she'd become to him, but he felt she knew. As he moved within her it was as if he could read her thoughts, feeling the sacred bond only lovers possessed.

This night was different than the first. She trusted him, and he returned that trust. Her shyness was gone, and she met his every thrust with one of her own. He was lost in emotions he could no longer control. She was his, of that he was sure.

Tonight belonged to them, to share and to love. And when he returned, he'd find a way to make every night belong to them. No more empty feelings and sleeping alone. He wanted her by his side, in his bed, for the rest of their lives.

10

"PREGNANT?" Jake stared wide-eyed.

"Yes, you're going to be a papa." Princess laid her head on Jake's shoulder and sighed. "That must be why I've had all these strange cravings lately."

"Pregnant?" He sounded like a record stuck in the same groove.

She nudged his chin with her nose. "Isn't it wonderful, Monsieur?"

"Pregnant?"

"Quit babbling like an idiot. *Oui, oui,* you silly goose. Tiny babies. More than one."

Jake strutted around her and scratched at the grass. "Are you sure?"

"Look at me!" She jumped to her hind feet and exposed her poochy belly.

Jake sat on his haunches. "Hey, hey! Don't be doin' that. You might strain something. Aren't mothers-to-be supposed to take it easy?"

She rubbed her face against his. "You old softy."

"Just lie down here and rest. When's these kids supposed to pop out?"

"Any day now."

"Holy Moly." Jake swallowed hard. "A dad—I'm gonna be a dad any day now," he repeated. "Hey, wait right there. I've got something for you." He strutted to his side of the tree and trotted back with the bone he had hidden from her all these weeks. He dropped it at her feet.

She stared, then sniffed it. "Yuck! Where did you get that nasty old thing?"

"It's yours."

"Monsieur! I have never owned anything so disgusting in my life!"

He rolled the bone over with his paw. "I got it from your side of the tree."

She tossed her head haughtily. "It is *not* mine!"

"You mean I've been hiding that bone all this time and it ain't even yours?" He laid his head on his paws, sighing. "Women!"

"JENNY MCNEILL," Dave said, a smile as broad as Texas stretched across his face, "I'd like you to meet Megan Kasada."

Jenny stood in the open door of her cottage and stared at the little blond-headed, blue-eyed beauty standing next to Dave. His exuberance was contagious, and she found herself grinning. The smell of pepperoni seeped from the large pizza box he had in his hands.

"Come in, for heaven's sake." She gestured for them to enter, took the box from Dave and sat it on a nearby table. "So nice to meet you, Megan. Your dad has told me lots of wonderful things about you." She turned to Dave. "I'm glad you're back. I take it your trip was successful?" Her eyes searched his.

Had the meeting gone as he expected? Was Nancy demanding full custody of Megan?

She didn't think his smile could get any broader, but it did.

"You're not going to believe this—"

Jake darted into the kitchen, fell to his belly and slid to a stop in front of the table holding the pizza. He leaped up, sniffing.

"No, no, Jake." Megan patted the side of her leg for him to come. Jake wiggle-walked to her so hard he nearly fell over. "Look, Daddy, he remembers me!"

Dave squatted to pet the dog. "How's my buddy?" Jake answered with an affectionate lick on his cheek. He turned to smile at Jenny. "Thanks for watching him for me. Hope he wasn't any trouble."

"Not much," she conceded. She hated to admit it, but the darn dog was lovable.

Princess joined them and danced a circle on her hind feet, delighting Megan.

"Ooh, another puppy!" She held out her arms and Princess and Jake engaged in a licking contest.

Over giggles, yips and woofs, Dave herded Megan and the dogs toward the door. "Sweetie, why don't you go out and play with Princess and Jake while I talk to Jenny."

"Okay, Daddy. Then can we eat our pizza?"

He glanced at Jenny. "I should have called to see if you were busy."

Jenny smiled. "Never too busy to eat." *Or to see you*, her heart added.

He hurried Megan along. "We'll eat in a few

minutes, honey. Don't let the dogs tear up anything," he warned.

When he turned, his gaze locked with Jenny's. "I missed you." He reached for her hand.

His voice was soft, mesmerizing, his touch electrifying. Had he only been gone a few days? It had seemed like an eternity. She couldn't speak, couldn't tell him how much she missed him. Even if she could, what good would it do?

Finding her voice, she gently pulled away. "I've never seen you look happier. You weren't just spouting fatherly pride. Megan is beautiful."

"I am happy, Jenny—and I wanted to share it with you. You've been on my mind every moment since I left—"

"The pizza's getting cold," she interrupted, uncomfortable with the conversation. "Maybe we should call Megan inside. It looks like rain. I'll make some iced tea..." She faltered when she felt his hand touch her shoulder. When he pulled her to him, her body turned to mush and molded against his firm torso.

"Jenny," he whispered against her hair, "I couldn't wait to get back and tell you the good news. You're the one I wanted to share it with."

She buried her face in his shoulder, drawing close to his warmth. "I could use some good news."

Lifting her face, he brushed her cheek with the back of his finger, then slid his hand around her neck and lowered his head to kiss her. Her first instinct was to pull away, but her body betrayed her good judgment. Her lips invited his all too eagerly.

"God, I missed you."

His voice was low and breathy. She leaned into him and rested her cheek against his chest. She felt his steady heartbeat and even breathing. She had missed him, too.

"What's the good news?" she asked as she pulled away and moved toward the kitchen.

Dave picked up the pizza and followed her. "Nancy didn't want full custody of Megan. She wanted to reverse custody."

Jenny glanced up. "Reverse? What's that mean?"

"She wants Megan certain holidays and summer vacations only. Otherwise, Megan gets to stay with me."

"That's wonderful!"

"Isn't it? I can't believe it. I went to Chicago ready for battle. I had to read those damn papers her father drew up twice before it soaked in. I thought they were trying to pull another one over on me."

Throwing caution to the wind, Jenny flung her arms around him and hugged him tight. "Oh, Dave, that's wonderful! I really am happy for you."

"For once Nancy did something for the good of our child. She admitted her life-style would not be good for Megan, especially after school starts."

"And she agreed to just visitation?"

He nodded. "I'd never deprive Megan of seeing her mother, so I had the papers amended to give her more than she asked for. With notice, she can see Megan whenever she wants."

"How's Megan adjusting to the news?"

"That's what's so remarkable. This is what Megan

has wanted all along. Oh, don't get me wrong. She loves her mother. She just doesn't like traveling. She misses our time together. I play—Nancy shops.''

Jenny laughed. ''What is it they say? When the going gets tough, the tough go shopping.''

Dave slipped the pizza in the oven to warm. ''I'd like you to help me get Megan settled in school. You've lived here and know the ropes. I don't even know who to see about getting her started.''

Ice cubes crackled when she poured tea in the glasses. ''You go to the school and ask. They'll tell you what you have to do and the supplies you'll have to purchase.''

''Supplies?''

''Scissors, crayons, tablets. Dave, you're going to have to do this on your own.''

His brows raised.

''I have news, too.'' She placed plates, napkins and forks on the table. ''I'm leaving the island.''

Accepting a glass of tea, he gazed at her, his demeanor sobering. ''No luck finding suitable space?''

She shook her head. ''There's nothing.''

''There's got to be something. Let me see what I can do. I know how much you love it here.''

''Dave.'' She felt her courage draining. ''I hate to see my expansion plans go down the drain, but there's no place on the island for me to relocate.''

''I told you, if it's money—''

She held her hand up. ''No. I won't accept charity.'' The last thing she would do was take money from him.

He sat the glass down, then pulled the pizza out of

the oven and set it on the counter. Their hands brushed. "You could make me a partner, a silent backer."

That made her laugh. A partner? That wasn't what she wanted. She'd built Fudgeballs from scratch. She didn't need a partner. She wanted him for reasons entirely different. "Don't be silly. You didn't get where you are in the business world by doing charity work for misguided fudge makers."

"You aren't misguided. Believing what Hank Linstrom told you wasn't your fault." He put slices of pizza on plates. "I can move."

His voice was so low, so casual, she didn't catch what he said. "What?"

"I said I'll move. You stay on the island."

She shook her head. "I couldn't in clear conscience let you do that. You own the building. Your business is just as thriving as mine—"

"But you've lived here longer. This is your home."

"You love it here, too. You've said as much. Now you have Megan, and this is a wonderful place to bring up a child. No pollution, no—"

"No you."

"Dave." She was afraid to look at him, afraid she might cry. "Don't make this any harder than it is."

Megan burst into the room, squealing as Princess and Jake chased her. "Princess likes me, Jenny!"

Jenny put her arm around the child's shoulders and squeezed her close. "Who wouldn't?" Jenny felt a rush of warmth as Megan hugged her waist.

"You smell good," the little girl said.

Jenny kissed the top of her head. "Come with me. I'll make you smell good, too."

She took Megan into her bedroom and spritzed Chanel behind each of her ears. The girl beamed and held her hair off her neck.

"Here," Jenny said, "let me put it in a ponytail. Then your daddy can smell your perfume."

Megan fiddled with Jenny's makeup on the dresser while her hair was being tied with a bow. "Can I put some lipstick on?"

"Why not?" Jenny said. "Need help?"

Megan handed the tube to her. As she applied gloss to the child's lips, shivers ran down her arms. It would be so easy to fall in love with Dave's daughter—as much in love as she was with him.

Megan pressed her lips together and studied her image in the mirror. "Do I look beautiful?"

"Absolutely." Jenny straightened. "Let's go show you off to your daddy."

"Yeah. I love my daddy."

Yeah, Jenny thought. *So do I.*

A WEEK LATER, Jenny closed a box, then taped it shut. Straightening, she supported the small of her back. Moving would be a lot easier if her heart was in it. The cramped business space she'd rented in Mackinac City could only be considered downsizing. Without the island trade, business would fall off. It would be months, years before she could think about expanding. Winter was coming, and with the island isolated from the mainland during bad weather, she would be forced to give up her cottage and move across the lake.

Sitting on the box, she looked around her. The shop was starting to look empty. It wasn't only business that bothered her. Dave was on her mind constantly. She couldn't accuse him of betrayal, though she wanted to. She was as guilty as he was for the misunderstanding. She laughed. Their farcical circumstances gave new meaning to the phrase *lack of communication.*

Tears welled in her eyes when she thought of all that might have been. Megan had taken to her instantly, and she to Megan. Why couldn't she bury her pride, accept Dave's offer to stay on the island, see where the relationship would go from here?

She blew her nose. *Life stinks.*

"We're down to the last crate." Mrs. Wilcox emerged from the back room. "And there's just a few small boxes left."

"I'll have to get more tomorrow." Jenny got up, wiping her eyes. "You can quit for the day, Mrs. Wilcox. I'm tired. I want to go home."

Mrs. Wilcox put her hands on her ample hips. "You sure, dearie? The mister said he didn't mind if I stayed late."

"There's no need." The season was winding down. The Labor Day Bridge Walk, which drew over a hundred thousand people, had come and gone. Fewer tourists were visiting the shop now that school had started.

A chilly rain started to fall as Jenny locked up for the night. She refused to look toward the kite shop.

She'd avoided Dave lately. A clean break was the only sensible one. She noticed Jake wasn't tied to the tree. Dave must have taken him inside because of the rain.

Princess had seemed listless this morning, so she had left her home, leaving the doggy door unlatched so she could come and go if necessary.

As she pedaled home, tears mingled with raindrops, blinding her at times. Images of Dave's smile, Megan with eyes so like her father's, visions of the three of them as a family unit, the sound of Dave's laughter, the touch of his hand, the feel of his kiss, the whisper of his needy voice when they made love...

She slipped her key in the lock and opened the door to the cottage. A rush of damp air greeted her. ''Princess? I'm home.'' She moved through the dark cottage, switching on lights while searching for matches, hoping a cheery fire would chase away the blues.

Passing the bedroom, she paused, listening to faint mewlings on the opposite side of the door. Nudging the door open wider, her jaw dropped when she saw Jake and Princess in Dory's cradle surrounded by three tiny, squirming forms.

She broke into a grin, moving swiftly to the bedside. ''Why, Jake, you rascal.'' She picked up the smallest puppy, stroking its damp fur, still damp from birthing. The newborns couldn't be more than a few hours old. She glanced at Jake. ''How did you get in here?''

Jake sat up, panting. *The puppy trapdoor, human. Sorry to intrude, but my woman needed me. We used the Lamaze method.*

"Princess." Jenny gently patted the tired mother. "I never dreamed—you *were* putting on weight!"

The babies mewled and scrambled over each other, rooting for their dinner. One looked exactly like Jake, jutted jaw and pug-faced, while the other two strongly favored their mother.

Jenny set the boy in the crib, then examined the two squirming white ones. Two girls and a boy. She beamed with pride. She was a grandmother!

Hugging one of the females to her breast, she dropped to her knees, overcome with emotion. She was bawling over puppies, for gosh sake! She wanted babies of her own—with Dave. Memories rushed back, memories of picnics and ferry rides in his arms. No matter how many times she told herself they were ill-suited for each other, her heart told her they were made for each other.

Why was she being so pigheaded? Why didn't she just admit she loved him and make her life a whole lot easier? Her misgivings melted like ice cream on a hot sidewalk. What the heck. You only lived—and truly loved—once.

She reached for the phone. She was tired of fighting feelings that no longer made any sense. There would be problems to overcome, but together, she and Dave could do it.

"Dave?" She bit her lip. She'd gone too long without hearing his voice.

"I was wondering of you'd ever get around to calling."

"Don't say anything. Just..." She bit back tears. "Just come over, will you?"

"Give me ten minutes to close the store and pick up Megan from the sitter."

She hung up, wiping tears from the corners of her eyes. She was going to feel pretty foolish if he didn't share her sentiments.

Seven and a half minutes later, his knock shook the door. When she opened it, Megan and Dave were standing in front of her. She walked into his arms, catching Megan around the waist to form a family circle.

Holding each other, they rocked back and forth. The smell of his after-shave washed over her, flooding her with sensual memories.

"Jenny?"

"Shhh," she whispered. "We were both wrong."

"I'd do anything to—"

"It doesn't matter. I should have told you what I was planning to do."

His mouth found hers with a long, hungry kiss. They had been apart too long, much too long to be separated from love.

Jake barked, demanding attention.

Lifting his head, Dave frowned. "Was that Jake? He slipped out of his collar again. I figured he was in the pound."

"Jake?" Megan broke away, skipping toward the barking sound. "Jake! Where are you, boy?"

Taking Dave by the hand, Jenny pulled him inside. "I think your dog has something he needs to get off his chest."

"What's he doing here?"

Jenny pulled him along the hallway, pausing before

the doorway to the guest room. Behind the door a lot of mewling and barking was going on.

Megan pressed closer. "What's that sound?"

Dave's brows knitted in the middle of his forehead. "Sounds like a kennel in there."

Jenny pushed the door open, then stood back to allow Dave's and Megan's entrance. His eyes followed the noisy sounds emulating from the cradle, a smile gradually spreading across his features. The puppies were crying, their eager mouths searching for their mother.

As Dave approached, Jake sat up straighter, wagging his tail.

Dave's gaze focused on the squirming puppies, and he shook his head. "Well, I'll be damned, Jake. What have you done?"

"Look, Daddy!" Megan bounced up and down. "Jake's got puppies!"

Princess lifted her head, her gentle eyes sweeping her children. Nudging the runt closer with her nose, she settled him at her teats.

Megan's little hands gently moved the babies closer to their source of milk.

Jenny approached from behind, slipping her hand into Dave's. They watched the newborns, awed and inspired by the familial sight. "I figure this makes us grandparents," she whispered.

Dave laughed, pulling her tightly to him. His embrace said that for the moment it was enough to be in each other's arms.

"I've *really* missed you," he whispered.

She was so choked with emotion, all she could do

was kiss him. She poured her feelings into the response. There was so much she wanted to say, so very much.

Setting her away slightly, he gazed into her eyes. The love he saw shining in the depths was strong and unmistakable. "I want to make a bargain with you."

Her fingers lightly brushed a lock of hair from his forehead. He had such beautiful, expressive eyes. "I'm listening."

"I've spent the last two days drawing up plans. If I can get clearance, I'm adding a second story to the building."

She tensed, willing to forgive him, but the eviction still smarted, no matter how nice he was about it.

"Don't tense up on me." Pulling her closer, he whispered, "Aren't you going to ask why?"

She met his firm, even gaze. "I don't need to. You're expanding the store."

His gaze softened. "Yes and no. I'm taking over the upstairs, and I thought if I asked real nice—" he kissed the tip of her nose "—you might agree to keep Fudgeballs downstairs. If you're agreeable, I'd like to franchise Fudgeballs—make it a big part of Rockfield. Between kites and fudge, we should be able to make ends meet, don't you think?"

Her pulse jumped. He was asking her to stay on, to keep Fudgeballs on the island, to go on with her expansion? She started to tremble, and he took both her hands, bringing them to his chest.

She searched for her voice. "That sounds more like a compromise. What's the bargain?"

"The bargain is, marry me and you won't have to pay monthly rent."

Her jaw dropped, and he gently tapped it closed. "Of course, I'll be getting the better deal. You'll be momma to Megan, and love slave and domestic goddess to me—"

She giggled at his baloney.

"I want you as my partner, Jenny. My life's partner. I need you. I love you."

"Me, too, Jenny. And I like candy," Megan said, hugging Jenny around the waist.

His features sobered as he threaded his fingers through Jenny's. "The bargain is mine. I want to start over with you, no lies, no misunderstandings, just total, complete surrender of love."

"Oh, Dave." The answer was so simple. "Yes, yes, a thousand, thousand times yes."

He captured her mouth in a kiss that made all rational thought escape. There would be time to say how much she loved him. She would grow to love his daughter. Even time to accept Jake, a natural addition to the family now that he and Princess had three extra mouths to feed.

There would be time for that, and more, but not now. She snuggled closer, surrendering to all he offered.

"BEAUREGARDE? Never!" Jake snorted. "No pup of mine is going to be named Beauregarde."

"That is a perfectly acceptable French name."

"Why, he'd be the laughingstock of the neighborhood. There wouldn't be a dog on the island that wouldn't pick a fight with him." He kicked at the grass with his hind foot. "What's wrong with Butch? Or Jake Junior?"

"Beauregarde," Princess insisted.

"Hey, I never squawked at the girls' names—Fifi and Mimi—but I'm naming my boy."

"Now, don't make a fuss. We're naming *our* boy Beauregarde." Princess snuggled close and wiggled her hindquarters against him.

"Jake Junior."

"Beauregarde."

She wiggled again, and his amorous side betrayed him. "Hoo, boy." He licked the top of her head. She pressed closer, and he put his front leg over her.

She let out a long breath. "I love you, *Monsieur.*"

Women! He smacked his chops. "Aw...shucks. I love you, too, Frenchie. Could we at least just call the little feller Beau?"

Take 4 bestselling love stories FREE

a FREE surprise gift!

Special Limited-time Offer

Mail to Harlequin Reader Service®

3010 Walden Avenue
P.O. Box 1867
Buffalo, N.Y. 14240-1867

YES! Please send me 4 free Harlequin Love and Laughter™ novels and my free surprise gift. Then send me 4 brand-new novels every other month, which I will receive months before they appear in bookstores. Bill me at the low price of $2.90 each plus 25¢ delivery per book and applicable sales tax if any*. That's the complete price and a savings of over 10% off the cover prices— quite a bargain! I understand that accepting the books and gift places me under no obligation ever to buy any books. I can always return a shipment and cancel at any time. Even if I never buy another book from Harlequin, the 4 free books and the surprise gift are mine to keep forever.

102 BPA A7EF

Name	(PLEASE PRINT)	
Address	Apt. No.	
City	State	Zip

This offer is limited to one order per household and not valid to present Love and Laughter™ subscribers. *Terms and prices are subject to change without notice. Sales tax applicable in N.Y.

ULL-397   ©1996 Harlequin Enterprises Limited

DEBBIE MACOMBER

invites you to the

★ HEART OF TEXAS ★

Join Debbie Macomber as she brings you the lives and loves of the folks in the ranching community of Promise, Texas.

If you loved Midnight Sons—don't miss Heart of Texas! A brand-new six-book series from Debbie Macomber.

Available in February 1998 at your favorite retail store.

Heart of Texas by Debbie Macomber

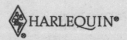

HARLEQUIN®

Welcome to *Love Inspired*™

A brand-new series of contemporary inspirational love stories.

Join men and women as they learn valuable lessons about facing the challenges of today's world and about life, love and faith.

**Look for the following April 1998
Love Inspired™ titles:**

DECIDEDLY MARRIED
by Carole Gift Page

A HOPEFUL HEART
by Lois Richer

HOMECOMING
by Carolyne Aarsen

Available in retail outlets in March 1998.

LIFT YOUR SPIRITS AND GLADDEN YOUR HEART
with *Love Inspired!*™

**Steeple
Hill**™

LI498

HARLEQUIN ULTIMATE GUIDES™

A series of how-to books for today's woman.

Act now to order some of these extremely
helpful guides just for you!

*Whatever the situation, Harlequin Ultimate Guides™
has all the answers!*

#80507	HOW TO TALK TO A	$4.99 U.S. ☐	
	NAKED MAN	$5.50 CAN.☐	
#80508	I CAN FIX THAT	$5.99 U.S. ☐	
		$6.99 CAN.☐	
#80510	WHAT YOUR TRAVEL AGENT	$5.99 U.S. ☐	
	KNOWS THAT YOU DON'T	$6.99 CAN.☐	
#80511	RISING TO THE OCCASION		
	More Than Manners: Real Life	$5.99 U.S. ☐	
	Etiquette for Today's Woman	$6.99 CAN.☐	
#80513	WHAT GREAT CHEFS	$5.99 U.S. ☐	
	KNOW THAT YOU DON'T	$6.99 CAN.☐	
#80514	WHAT SAVVY INVESTORS	$5.99 U.S. ☐	
	KNOW THAT YOU DON'T	$6.99 CAN.☐	
#80509	GET WHAT YOU WANT OUT OF	$5.99 U.S. ☐	
	LIFE—AND KEEP IT!	$6.99 CAN.☐	

(quantities may be limited on some titles)

TOTAL AMOUNT	$
POSTAGE & HANDLING	$
($1.00 for one book, 50¢ for each additional)	
APPLICABLE TAXES*	$ _____
TOTAL PAYABLE	$ _____

(check or money order—please do not send cash)

To order, complete this form and send it, along with a check or money
order for the total above, payable to Harlequin Ultimate Guides, to:
In the U.S.: 3010 Walden Avenue, P.O. Box 9047, Buffalo, NY
14269-9047; **In Canada:** P.O. Box 613, Fort Erie, Ontario, L2A 5X3.

Name: _____

Address: _____ City: _____

State/Prov.: _____ Zip/Postal Code: _____

*New York residents remit applicable sales taxes.
Canadian residents remit applicable GST and provincial taxes.

◆HARLEQUIN®

HNFBL4